"Lehman, a friend and colleague, has always been a thoughtful lay theologian. In *The Candleberry Tales*, he provides us with thoughtful, hilarious, and at times frustrating as well as challenging stories of Christian daily-life interactions. Humanizing and humorizing the situations of Christian leaders and congregations, Lehman dares the readers to think about God, sources of authority, congregational structures and community, institutional despair and hope, and the mystery of God in stories. English is not my native language, but I was able to follow the stories—their humor and challenges—and enjoy a time of theological reflection in an inter-cultural mode of thinking. I will certainly include some of these stories in my under-graduate classes as examples of story-telling theological reflections taking our emotions from laughter to intrigue and curiosity."

—CARLOS F. CARDOZA ORLANDI,
Frederick E. Roach Chair in World Christianity Studies, Baylor University

"Karl Lehman in *The Candleberry Tales* using his keen humor invites us to look at the Gospel in a fresh way. We are reminded that while our religious experiences may be messy and may look different for each of us, it continues to be an important part of one's life. He also reminds us, as we read the journey of each character, that not only is it okay to have a sense of humor as we travel our own religious journey, a sense of humor may be necessary."

—JUANITA STEDMAN, Executive Director, Together Georgia

"*The Candleberry Tales* has something of Chaucer's wit and satire, poking fun at the eccentricities of those who presume to represent Christianity in our day. As with Chaucer, Lehman invites us to consider the varieties of religious experience in the church—or, rather, the churches—with their manifest foibles and eccentricities on full display. In these updated tales we meet the twelve 'Early County O'Postles' on the road in a dilapidated old church bus, bound not for glory but for Camp Candleberry. As they share their tales, we discover their pieties and proclivities with their often delightful—if not also absurd—consequences. Along the way Lehman leaves no one unscathed, rendering every member of this ecumenical troupe with a suitable levity. These Tales serve as a reminder—if we needed one—that those who take up the mantle of ministry are no different than those who endure their sermons week by week, all of us—depending on your point of view—as delightful as we are ridiculous. Together, they exemplify the truth that the ongoing existence of the church and its ministers, on fulsome display here, is reason enough to believe in God's patience or humor—and probably both."

—MARK S. BURROWS, author of *Meister Eckhart's Book of Darkness and Light: Meditations on the Path of the Wayless Way*

"In his book, *The Candleberry Tales*, Karl Lehman weaves a captivating story about the annual journey of eleven rural pastors traveling on a wobbly school bus through rural Georgia, who each take turns sharing outlandish and highly humorous stories themed by a scriptural reference. I highly recommend that you join them on their journey as they reveal not only their eclectic theological beliefs, but a refreshing critique on the future of the twenty-first-century church."

—TOM HAGOOD, Pastor, Columbia Presbyterian Church, Decatur, Georgia

The Candleberry Tales

The Candleberry Tales

KARL D. LEHMAN

Foreword by Justo L. González

RESOURCE *Publications* · Eugene, Oregon

THE CANDLEBERRY TALES

Resource Publications
An Imprint of Wipf and Stock Publishers
199 W. 8th Ave., Suite 3
Eugene, OR 97401

www.wipfandstock.com

PAPERBACK ISBN: 979-8-3852-4602-1
HARDCOVER ISBN: 979-8-3852-4603-8
EBOOK ISBN: 979-8-3852-4604-5

05/05/25

For Ondina
Mi vida

Contents

Foreword
(or Forewarning?)

HOW DOES ONE WRITE a serious word about humor? To analyze humor is like dissecting a living body: it kills it! Humor is meant to be enjoyed, not to be studied, defined, classified, preserved . . . Therefore, before I go further into this Foreword, and before any more serious word about the present book, I must enthusiastically declare that, even apart of any other virtues, Lehman's stories are fun to read!

Yet, humor is a serious matter. It is serious because it is powerful. As any other human power, it can be used for both good and evil—and even for both at the same time. Laughing at others and casting ridicule on them is to dehumanize and even to destroy them. Despite the popular saying, a bully's words may hurt more than sticks and stones.

On the other hand, humor may be liberating by focusing attention on the cracks of oppressive "realities"; by debunking apparently inescapable "facts"; by turning this topsy-turvy world upside down—as perhaps it should be!

As we will see in the stories that follow, one the greatest virtues of humor is that it does not have to be believable, nor even credible. In these humorous stories, a mouse can be a theologian (perhaps also in actual fact, but that is another matter); and the unattainable dream may be achieved and then prove a failure.

Humor is able to challenge the comfort zones in which we trim our values so not to carry them through their ultimate consequences. It can challenge the present use of supposedly specialized bibles for what is really profiteering—and do so without fear of being sued. It can question and challenge privilege. And it can also be fun, as is the case with all the stories in this book.

Humor has the freedom to be polysemic, to speak to different issues at the same time. "Church in the Sky," for instance, may be read as directed against uncommunicative and incompetent church bureaucracies, or as addressing the tendency of churches to live in isolation from the rest of the world.

Humor has one foot firmly on the ground of reality, and another in the clouds of imagination. Good nonsense makes its own sense. It is in this nonsensical sense that humor becomes both a challenge to what is taken for granted, and a harbinger of undreamt possibilities.

But above all, humor sheds new and different lights on well-traveled dead-end alleys, such as the never-ending debates about differing interpretations of the Bible. In the story "West of Eden," a brief dialogue does precisely that: To Ron's comment that "We've got a big Bible. There's room in it for everybody," Bob replies: "No, Ron, I think it's too big for anybody."

That dialogue leads me to imagine the Holy Spirit telling the heavenly host: "Don't be surprised that I decided to inspire four different Gospels, even though they disagree on so many details. If those Christians had only one Gospel, they would imagine that they were possessors of all truth, as if they could carry it in their pockets. But when they think they have all the answers in Matthew, I hit them with something else in Luke. And if they memorize John, I chastise them with something different from Mark. I just want to keep them listening! I hope that by listening to me they will get better at listening to one another."

In short, to speak of the divine, to think of the divine, to worship the divine, a bit of humor is not amiss.

This seems to be the view of an (imaginary) ancient manuscript recently discovered in a cave on Mt. Ahranin, and not readily available to the public because ancient Armaetic is difficult to understand. After much research, and with some hesitation, I dare suggest that the document should be entitled "The Bedtime Stories that Miriam Told Her Baby Brother Moses in the House of Pharaoh."

Some excerpts are worth quoting as being relevant to our subject:

> In the beginning, when earth was without form, and void,
> the spirit of God smiled over the face of the waters.
> And the waters smiled back.

Laughing, God said, "Let there be light."
    And the light laughed over the face of the earth.
And God sang the name of all things.
    And all things, leaping into existence, sang back.
And God said, "Let us make humans after our image."
    And humans danced with God.
And God saw that it was all God. And God smiled, and laughed,
and sang, and danced.
Upon hearing this, baby Moses giggled.
    And in his giggle shone the grace of God.

Justo L. González
Decatur, GA
Mardi Gras, 2025

The Prologue

"HEY EVERYBODY! LET'S GO!" Dave Tucker was getting mighty impatient. Standing in front of Sam's Diner in Blakely, Georgia, the Methodist minister was yelling at his colleagues through the old restaurant's wooden screened door.

"Man! It's only April and already too stinking muggy and hot," Dave cursed to himself. He stuck his head inside the door and, being a tall man, he got himself caught in some of those strips of yellow fly paper dangling from the tin ceiling. "It's time to go!" he yelled again, pulling the sticky strips from his hair.

Squeezed into a maroon Naugahyde booth, eleven Early County ministers slurped the last drops of coffee, grabbed the remaining donuts, and darted for the door. Outside, they wasted no time and hopped aboard the old church bus that was the pride of Rev. Tucker's fleet. He bragged it had been used on a television show back in the early seventies. If you looked closely enough, you could still detect the word *Partridge* beneath the hand-painted Early Methodist Church sign on its side.

Seated on faded psychedelic seats, a few with loose springs, the bantering "Twelve O'Postles," as they called themselves, joyously broke into their song. It followed the tune of that famous hymn, "Amazing Grace," and all but one knew it by heart:

> Big disgrace,
> How bad we sound
> We'll make all pews unused!
> And everyone,
> At rapture time
> Will wish we stayed behind!

When they finished their song and all were settled into their seats, Rev. Tucker led everybody in prayer: for the world-wide church, the president, the governor, for home-bound parishioners, for ecumenical harmony, and lastly, for the bus's nineteen seventies transmission. With a loud "Amen," Dave cranked up the engine, popped the clutch, and stomped on the bus's foot-shaped accelerator.

Blam, pop, sputter, blam! The old diesel engine coughed, backfired, and engulfed the diner and everything else along the block in a choking purple haze of billowing smoke. After two or three whiplash jolts, the bus lurched onto Blakely's Main Street and started that long pilgrimage from deepest South Georgia to Camp Candleberry, near the mountains of Chattooga, in the state's sparsely developed northwestern corner.

Camp Candleberry was at one time speculative investment property owned by one Nelson Bunker Candleberry, a Cartersville business tycoon who lost his fortune in a foolhardy attempt at forging a monopoly on dry communion wafers. His bankruptcy agreement required that he donate the property to a worthy charity. Being a devout Methodist, he gave it to the church along with two thousand cases of unsold communion wafers. Nelson jokingly called Camp Candleberry his "vestment property."

To reach the camp, the Twelve O'Postles always followed the long and winding state route 27. It took them clear around Cuthbert, skirting Columbus, and bypassing Newnan, Cartersville, and Rome. By sunset they would reach Camp Candleberry on the top side of Summerville, ten miles from Trion as a hungry buzzard flies.

Aside from the semi-retired Rev. Tucker, the Twelve O'Postles included the slightly right-of-center Jim Mayer, and Sue Moyers, herself a wee bit left-of-center. Like Dave, these folks were Methodist, though while in college Jim thought he was sort of an atheist. There was also a trio of Baptist preachers: Billy Barker, an expert in family values; the prophecy-focused Ben Boyle (his friends jokingly called him Rev. Flame Thrower); and Bob Bending, a man leaning towards the Cooperative Baptist Fellowship. Also joining the group was southwest Georgia's lone Lutheran pastor, Ken Lesley, the easy-going Christian Church preacher, Ron Morgan; a high-church Episcopalian rector, Sarah Priestly; and her overly orderly cousin. Named May Presley, she was Presbyterian, as was the blue-blooded Princeton Newport III, who joined them this year. Finally, there was one independent preacher, a former mortgage banker named Ed Steale.

Along the way from Sam's Diner to Camp Candleberry, each preacher told a tale he or she had spun, some prepared weeks in advance and a few on-the-spot. Much like parables but not too preachy, these stories all had a moral and brought light to a thing or two Jesus had said. Instead of drawing toothpicks, the Twelve drew left-over palm branches. Having pulled the shortest one, Rev. Sue Moyers said, "I'm first! She stepped to the front of the bus.

"Then let's hear your tale!" Rev. Tucker said.

"Right," Sue replied. "My text is from John's Gospel, the sixth chapter and thirty-second verse: 'It was not Moses who gave you bread from heaven.'" She took a deep breath and then began her tale. "It's the story of Harvey Stilton, a Presbyterian preacher." She continued, "A preacher who rediscovered God's spirit within!"

"Amen, Sue!" Billy Barker cheered.

"Go, girl!" May yelled.

With that last comment, Sue began her tale.

Rev. Harvey Stilton and His Truly Amazing Machine

Then Jesus said, "Very truly, I tell you, it was not Moses who gave
you the bread from heaven, but it is my Father who gives you the
true bread from heaven.

(JOHN 6:32, NRSV)

"DECENTLY, IN ORDER, AND with utmost efficiency," Rev. Harvey Stilton
would tell his parishioners again and again.

Enter his study, and you step into a world illuminated by the men
and women who gave their lives in service to humankind's endless struggle
against inefficiency. Perched on the mantel high above the fireplace is a
portrait of the person who, to Harvey, was the greatest one of them all:
Mary Anderson, inventor of the swinging arm windshield wiper now used
in nearly every truck and car the world over. Move deeper into the office
and you will see scores of pictures and statuettes of other famous and not-
so-famous inventors on the walls or scattered about on the tables and book-
shelves. Within this room Rev. Harvey Stilton can submerge himself in that
vast sea of collective genius possessed by these giants of the patent pending.
To Harvey, their creativity and inquisitiveness is a model for ministry he
has followed for nearly forty years.

With all the discipline of a Mary Anderson or even a Thomas Alva Edison, through each of these four decades, Rev. Stilton has stuck religiously to an unbending weekly schedule. In this calendar, Wednesday mornings belong to Harvey alone. Once each week, Harvey will disconnect his phone, turn off the electric typewriter, and lock away the appointment calendar in the top drawer of his century old oak desk. Madeline Rottweiler, the church secretary for as long as anyone can remember, serves as his indomitable gatekeeper. For her, a crisis sufficiently dire or urgent to warrant disturbing our Rev. is a rare occurrence indeed. She can recall having to do so just three times during the minister's entire tenure with the First Presbyterian Church of Hooperton.

When Harvey is alone in his idea-incubating study, his cup of creative genius runneth over. Twenty years ago on a Wednesday morning, Rev. Stilton hatched a new design for the offering plate. The brass, red-velvet-lined, bowl-shaped plate never made sense to him. By the time the ushers returned to the altar, the offering plates were, on a good Sunday, a chaotic mess of checks, cash, envelopes, notes, and loose change, an egregious affront to his sense of decency, order, and utmost efficiency. In his upper-room workshop, Harvey constructed a rectangular shellacked wooden offering plate with small compartments—for checks, for cash, for envelopes, for loose change, and for miscellanea. Actually, his offering organizer was Harvey's twenty-third patent. It was only five years ago that Rev. Harvey Stilton conceived of his most ingenious, most stupendous time-saving device of all: the incomparable Roto-Sermon machine.

Alone that Wednesday morning, several years ago, Harvey had a brilliant idea. "I could automate the production of sermons!" he declared with excitement.

First, Harvey wrote seven sermons of identical length. Each sermon was divided into seven equally sized, sequentially numbered paragraphs. Using his electric typewriter, Rev. Stilton typed each paragraph on a large card, and to the back of each card he affixed Velcro. He then designed and built a great machine of pulleys and seven parallel conveyor belts. The sermon cards were affixed to the conveyor belts: Each of the seven first paragraphs were attached to the first belt, each of the seven second paragraphs to the second belt, and so forth. With the turn of a lever, various cogged gears would move the seven parallel belts, each at different speeds. Thus, with the first rotation, paragraph one would move one place, paragraph two would move two places, paragraph three, four places, paragraph four, eight places, and so on for paragraphs five, six, and seven. Through this ingenious use of independently moving paragraph-laden conveyor belts, the seven sermons could be re-arranged into thousands of sermons and would last the minister a very, very, long time. To Rev. Stilton, this invention was not entirely unlike Jesus feeding five thousand men plus women and children with five loaves of bread and two fish.

After half a decade, Harvey was ready to tweak his Roto-Sermon machine. Aside from updating a few of the interchangeable paragraphs, Rev. Stilton had not needed to write another sermon, but now it was time to incorporate the common lectionary into this conveyor-belt system. The arithmetic calculation needed to match the three-year cycle of biblical texts with the seven independently moving paragraph-laden belts, each moving at different rotation cycles, was a challenge of Euclidean proportions. Harvey was confident he could figure it out.

One morning Harvey was in his normally peaceful study intently focused on solving the arithmetic-lectionary problem when the roar of construction equipment and loud banging noises outside interrupted his concentration. Curious, he got up and wandered over to the window to see what the ruckus was all about.

Across the street, Rev. Jimmy Splatterdash was directing the installation of a new sign for the mushrooming Victory Bible Temple and Christian Family Life Center. Rev. Stilton was astonished at the sheer size of the sign. Affixed to a steel post and thrusting some three-hundred feet into the air, the sign itself was almost twice the size of the Hooperton High School multi-purpose athletic field. It reminded Harvey of the gas station signs one sees along remote interstate highways. The sign was bright orange and illuminated by powerful halogen lights. In bold blue letters it simply read, "RU4–10." Harvey was befuddled.

"What in Heaven's name is he up to?"

At 4:00 pm the Rev. Stilton packed up his Roto-Sermon machine calculations in his briefcase and headed outside to his car, one of the last Checker Marathons to roll off the assembly line before that company's intractable resistance to modernity ran out of gas. Over at the Victory Bible Temple and Christian Family Life Center, Harvey could see Rev. Splatterdash and a group of people encircling the new signpost with their heads bowed and their hands linked.

"What in heaven's name are they doing?" he wondered as he backed out of his reserved parking space and headed towards home.

Along the way he stopped at Hooper's Farm-To-You Groceries. This being a Wednesday, his daughter, Mary Anderson Stilton, was dropping by for dinner, as was her custom ever since Harvey's wife had passed away a decade ago. Mary Anderson needed her dad to pick up some ingredients for a new recipe she had invented.

Inside Hooper's, Rev. Stilton quickly located the needed items and darted to the check-out line. He noticed that the cashier was wearing a small orange button with blue letters. As the line progressed and he got a bit closer to the register, he realized the clerk was wearing a miniature of the sign he had seen being erected earlier in the day. Her button read, "RU4-10."

"She must be involved with Jimmy's church," he thought.

Back in his Checker, the Revered Stilton continued the journey home. Along the way he saw several homes with orange and blue "RU4-10" signs; some affixed to mailboxes, some stapled to wooden stakes in yards, and still others taped to windows. Harvey also counted eleven minivans, sports utility vehicles, and station wagons with bumper-sticker versions of that same sign.

"Man, those things are everywhere!" Harvey said aloud, shaking his head.

"Were you able to get the stuff I needed?" Mary Anderson asked her dad as she walked over to the Checker. Harvey had just pulled into his driveway, and his daughter who had arrived a few minutes earlier, was waiting patiently.

"Yup," Harvey said. He got out of his car and handed Mary the brown Hooper's Farm-To-You paper bag bearing the store's trademark laughing carrot. "By the way," he asked her, "have you seen any of those RU4-10 signs?"

"I noticed the guy at the gas station had it on a pin he was wearing. My neighbor has one in her front yard, too. What do they mean?"

"It's something to do with that Jimmy Splatterdash," Harvey said. "They installed this huge RU4-10 sign today at his Victory Bible Temple. It's on a post several hundred feet high!" He raised his hands high in the air for emphasis. "Then they had some kind of prayer rally."

Mary Anderson and Harvey went through a side door of the house that opened directly into a large pantry. Harvey opened the door and instantaneously the overhead lights came on, and three racks for holding grocery bags sprung from a counter-top mini-garage he had designed and patented.

"Well, it worked the first time I tried it," Mary said. She and her dad were finishing their post-dinner glasses of Pepto-Bismol. "Sorry about that. I'm glad you had this on hand," she said apologetically.

"Look, you have your mother's adventurous spirit." Harvey put an arm around his daughter. "That's one of the things I so adored about her, and you for that matter. I enjoy being your guinea pig. The beans were just a bit spicy."

After cleaning up the kitchen, they headed for the family room to catch the evening news program. Mary snapped her fingers, and on came the television. Harvey called this invention the "Snapper." After an animated singing carrot commercial for Hooper's Farm-To-You Groceries, Mary and Harvey stopped their conversation and stared at the television. It wasn't a news flash that caught their attention. No, it was the Rev. Jimmy Splatterdash.

There he was, Jimmy Splatterdash wearing his trademark gold double-breasted satin suit. Behind him was a replica of the Ten Commandments chiseled into a block of granite that looked as if it had come from Stonehenge. He was pointing at the camera and, by inference, the viewer. "They have expelled God from the schoolhouse!" he bellowed. He pounded his fist on a clear plastic lectern, "and our nation has become a jail house! They flushed God out of the state house! And our nation has become an outhouse!" Rev. Splatterdash turned to face a different camera angle and continued his tirade. "Now is the time to stand up for God and his commandments. Not next year. Not next month. Not next week. And not even tomorrow. Now is the time!" He shook his fist in the air. "Stand with me as I take a stand for the Ten Commandments. Are you for them? If not, you are against them. Call me today at 1–555–444–1010 and I will send you this orange and blue pin." He held one of his RU4–10 pins in the air for a close-up shot. "By wearing this here pin, you'll show the world that you are on God's side!"

Then, "RU4–10" was flashing on the screen. A deep-baritone voice repeated the words,
"Are you for the Ten Commandments? If not, you are against them."

Like frightened opossums, Mary Anderson and Harvey couldn't move, nor could they utter a word. After several minutes they looked at each other and then back at the TV screen.

Harvey was first to regain some composure. "My word," he said. "No wonder everyone's acting so crazy. That man is starting to frighten me."

Besides the Wednesday time of solitude, Harvey's rigid schedule included three time periods for member visitations. Monday mornings were dedicated to visiting the sick. Last week Harvey had spent several hours with Hooperton banker Sterling Hogg who was briefly bedridden with an overdrawn checking account. He, too, had seen Jimmy Splatterdash on television.

"The thought of that man causes me great consternation," the banker told Rev. Stilton. "I think he's dangerous."

"Let's not overreact," Harvey replied. "He can't be that bad."

"I'm overreacting, you say?" Sterling exclaimed, a little angry. "That man's already been siphoning off our biggest contributors. And now he's even on the television!"

Tuesday afternoons were for family dysfunction. This past Tuesday a long-suffering Harvey had waded through three arduous hours of discussion with Holstina McCudd and her parents, Angus and Guernsey. They wanted to set a wedding date for Holstina and to talk to the Rev. Stilton about using First Presbyterian Church for both the service and reception. In Harvey's mind, the fact that Holstina had neither fiancé nor beau made setting a date problematic.

"Never you mind 'bout that, ole Angus gonna git her one tomorra," Holstina's father repeated over and over in his raspy voice.

Guernsey cut in, "Rev. Jimmy Splatterdash says women need to be with a husband. Our wee Holstina's gotta have one! It says so in the Bible."

"I don't think we should overreact," Harvey counseled. "I can't believe that the Rev. Splatterdash meant that literally."

"Overreact, us?" Guernsey and Angus said in unison.

"If you won't set a weddin' date for our wee Holstina, we'll have to go to Jimmy's church," Guernsey declared.

On Thursdays the Rev. Stilton could always be found with First Presbyterian's senior citizens. For the last seven years this occasion included lunch with Gertie Broiler, a woman just shy of her hundredth birthday. Old enough not to care, Gertie was described by most members as overly outspoken.

Shaking a gnarled cane at the television set, she growled, "I saw that pastor Jimmy on the TV yesterday evenin'. I don't trust that man, Rev. You watch out!"

Harvey helped Gertie off her rocker and carefully escorted her over to a chair at the kitchen table.

"I don't know what the Rev. Splatterdash is up to, Gertie. But I am concerned about it," he said.

"Rev., I been 'round here a long while. I seen the likes a' him before. Folks flock to 'em all the time. You ever hear of that preacher Willie Swank?"

"No, Gertie," Harvey said. "I don't think I have."

"Well, back in 19 and 35 he got everybody all riled up about them Rockettes. Made everybody think the world was comin' to an end. He kept talkin' 'bout how them Romans went belly-up when everybody started wearin' shorts. Turns out he got himself a new Lincoln with the money that was 'sposed to go to feedin' orphan kids, and then he fled to Valdosta and started somethin' over there."

"Maybe the Rev. Splatterdash will go away, too."

"Oh, I don't know 'bout that, Rev. I think you better do somethin' now!"

At 2:00 pm Harvey left Gertie's apartment. He got into his Checker, started up the car, and backed out of his parking space. It was getting dark and cloudy, and thunder was rumbling; a major storm was in the making. In the distance he could still see Gertie standing in her doorway shaking her wooden cane over her head. Though he couldn't hear her, he knew she was telling him to beware of Jimmy Splatterdash. It struck Harvey that the Mrs. Broiler with her cane in the air looked a bit like Moses parting the vast Red Sea. He pulled into the traffic and headed back to the First Presbyterian.

The church council's monthly meeting was the longest running of the church's regularly scheduled events. For ninety-three years it had always met on the first Sunday of each month at exactly 6:45 pm, with one exception. Back in December of 1941, most everyone stayed home to listen to President Roosevelt on the radio talking about war. The grandchildren of those who did show up still felt a little miffed over the earlier generation's lack of commitment to council meetings. Now, the council had to deal with a worrisome drop in attendance, and parishioners had been giving them all an earful.

"Holy cow, preacher! What you gonna do 'bout this?" Angus McCudd asked Harvey. He was feeling panicked. "You can't let our church die."

Madeline cut in, "You know as well as I do that everyone is going over to that Victory Bible Temple."

Youth leader and intern Ed Squirrels was eagerly raising his hand, trying to be noticed. "I've gotta an idea," he said in a way that Harvey thought was just a little too enthusiastic.

"Yes, Ed," Harvey said. "Tell us your idea."

"I think we should do our Messiah sing-along this month instead of at Christmas. Nobody ever does it in July. I'll bet a whole bunch a' people would come back."

"Nobody comes when we do it at Christmas," Madeline said sarcastically.

"Well, then, we might could do it bluegrass style," Ed shot back.

"They still ain't gonna come, Ed," Angus countered.

"I got another idea," Ed said, shaking his hand in the air. "What's that book about how your soul needs chicken soup? We might could do a cooking class with it."

"You idiot," Madeline barked. "It's not a cookbook."

"Those are good suggestions, Ed," Rev. Stilton said gently, briefly glaring at Ms. Rottweiler. "I don't believe we should rush into anything. We need to be in prayer and to consider carefully what God would have us do," he said, slowly and deliberately.

"That'll take too long preacher; we need action now," argued banker Sterling Hogg, feeling much better now that his account had some fresh deposits. "Long-term members create cash flow. We need'em back, and soon!"

"We're gonna run out of money," Madeline said abruptly. "I told every one of you not to buy those new hymnals. Those old ones were good enough."

After the meeting Harvey felt very discouraged and very bewildered. He wandered back to his office, ever so slowly. Once there, he closed the door, went to his desk, and fell back into the chair. He rubbed his temples with his index fingers. It seemed as if his church was deconstructing around him. Rev. Stilton looked up at the portrait of Mary Anderson.

"What have I done wrong?" he asked the portrait. "Where have I let these people down?" Then and there, Harvey decided to visit Jimmy's church in secret the next Sunday.

"I must see it for myself," he said resolutely. "Then I'll see things more clearly."

Wednesday evening came none too quickly for Rev. Harvey Stilton. He needed to be with his daughter. Like the week before, Mary Anderson had Harvey make a stop at Hooper's Farm-To-You Groceries on the way home.

At Hooper's he noticed more clerks wearing the orange and blue pins attached to their laminated name tags. Then, returning to his Checker, Harvey saw something stuck under the windshield wiper. It was an RU4–10 brochure. On the cover was Jimmy Splatterdash pointing at the reader. "Don't you be a coward too!" the brochure read, in bold typeface. Harvey opened the brochure. Inside were pictures of men in dark business suits taking Bibles from children and throwing them into green canvas bags. The text continued, "They took God from our schools. If you don't stand up for the Ten Commandments, they'll take your children too." On the back was a number to call, 1–555–444–1010, and a small picture of Jimmy Splatterdash. At the bottom were the words, "Your children are counting on you. I'm counting on you. God's counting on you. Call me today!" Harvey shook his head in disgust and tossed the brochure into the bag. He started up the Checker and headed home.

"Sorry Dad. Another bomb."

"Don't apologize. The beans were just a little too sour. One of these days you'll be ready for a patent." Mary Anderson smiled at that last comment. Harvey continued, "I wanted to talk to you about this RU4–10 thing again. You know, I've lost a lot of members to Jimmy Splatterdash and that Victory Bible Temple, and I'm getting a little concerned."

"My church is going through the same thing," Mary Anderson said. "The attendance dropped through the floor last month, and my pastor thinks we've lost nearly half our members to Rev. Splatterdash. She's more worried than you are."

"That Jimmy Splatterdash frustrates me so. He creates such an oppressive environment for everybody, but all he does is build up his membership with people from other churches. Next Sunday I've got a guest preacher coming, and I'm gonna attend that Victory Bible Temple to see it for myself."

Early Sunday morning Harvey withdrew to his bathroom. Thirty minutes later he emerged wearing a wig, fake beard, a borrowed suit, and glasses. Feigning an inability to speak English, he disguised himself as a vacationing Belgian believer eager to worship the Lord at the Victory Bible Temple and Christian Family Life Center.

Mary Anderson had dropped by on her way to church to see if he needed help. But when she saw her father, she burst out laughing.

"You look like Inspector Clouseau," she said, now on her knees unable to stand. "With a hat, I think it'll work." She got up and handed her father a beret she had borrowed from a friend. "I christen thee 'Jacques LeGume.'"

"I'll use that name," he said, taking the hat. "The hat too."

Harvey arrived at the Victory Bible Temple on foot. He had parked his car several blocks away for fear someone might recognize it, a wise move considering the fact that Harvey's was the only still-moving Checker Marathon registered in the Hooperton metro area.

Harvey joined a seemingly limitless throng of individuals and families heading up the hill to an enormous stadium-shaped church with an entryway of ten tall wooden doors, consecutively numbered with large chrome Roman numerals. Immediately inside the building there were ten turnstiles, and once through these, Harvey found himself in a narthex with bright red plush carpet and pearly white walls.

"I feel like I'm in Las Vegas," Harvey thought, looking at his surroundings. "Oh, my word," he said aloud.

Directly in front of Harvey were ten stone-tablet-shaped automated teller machines. Curious, he wandered over to them. Attached to each machine was a little sign that read, "Insert your Believer's Card® here." Next to this was a list of options:

    I.   Cash

    II.   Electronic Donations

   III.   Communion Kit

   IV.   Be Ye Blessed Message

    V.   Prayer Requests

   VI.   Pledges

  VII.   Love Offerings

 VIII.   RU4–10 Pins

  IX.   Signed Jimmy Photo

   X.   Commandment Cards

"Good God, I had no idea they were making such things," he thought, feeling both shocked and a little jealous. Harvey did not realize that a man in a green suit was standing right behind him.

"Hi, God loves you and I do too. I'm Nelson," the man said in a loud but mostly monotone voice. "You look familiar. Are you a visitor or do you normally go to the other side of our church?"

Startled, Harvey realized it was Nelson Lemming, one of his former members.

"No speaka no Eengleesh," Rev. Stilton replied. He noticed Nelson was wearing an orange and blue RU4-10 pin.

Loudly and very, very slowly Nelson asked, "Whaaat iiizzz yourrr naaaame?"

"Iya Jacques LeGume," Harvey said, doing his best both to hide his nervousness and to replicate a believable Belgian accent. "Iya go now, bye."

Trying to lose Nelson, Harvey turned and quickly entered the sanctuary, which to any first-time visitor was like wandering into the old Houston Astro Dome. He made his way up several flights of stairs until he was seated in one of the higher back-row pews.

"Lord, there's so many people you could spend a lifetime here and never recognize anyone," Harvey thought.

In the distance Harvey could see an altar, which actually was a large semi-circular stage. On the stage were a large clear-plastic pulpit, a long table against which was set yet another RU4-10 sign, ten very large chairs—that looked more like thrones—all arranged in one long row, and along the sides, two rectangular fountains, each with ten little geysers shooting up into the air. Behind the altar was a stepped choir loft consisting of ten gilded rows of pews.

By 10:45 the choir loft was filled, and at 10:59 the ten thrones were likewise filled. Harvey could make out Rev. Splatterdash sitting in one of the middle chairs. Seated next to Rev. Splatterdash was Mayor Bob Gander who, like Nelson, was a former member of First Presbyterian. Across the sanctuary he could also see a lot of other people who used to attend his church.

"Hi, Mister La Goom!"

Harvey looked to his left and was horrified to see Nelson Lemming sitting down next to him.

"Hiya," Harvey said, avoiding eye contact.

Mercifully, thought Harvey, the choir started singing, and three huge screens descended from the ceiling. At first they displayed successive camera shots of Jimmy Splatterdash, the other men on the altar, the choir, and lastly, images of people in the audience. Next, the words to a hymn appeared. Nelson and everyone in the congregation stood up and started swaying their arms in the air.

When the singing stopped, Jimmy Splatterdash walked up to the clear pulpit, opened his King James Bible and started reading some of the more gruesome selections of Deuteronomy, all the while doing his best to sound like an Old Testament prophet.

"The LORD will smite thee with the botch of Egypt and with the emerods, and with the scab, and with the itch, whereof thou canst not be healed." The text appeared on the suspended screens as well. Jimmy then looked sternly at the mass of people in the Victory Bible Temple, "Our God is no wimp. Longsuffering, the Bible says, but he's no wimp. And time is running out." Raising his Bible into the air, he yelled, "God gave us this book to obey. Those outside are a disobedient people and refuse to harken unto the laws of the LORD! But we have the power. We must take back this country for God before judgment falls upon this vile and wicked generation!"

With that last comment the audience again rose to its feet and in near unison cried, "Yes Jesus, give us the power!" Jimmy Splatterdash stepped down from the clear-plastic pulpit and sat in his throne-like chair.

Another of the pastors, Rev. Wayne Cheapjack, took a microphone in hand and sauntered over to the front row of seats. Wayne pulled a card from his vest pocket.

"I have a note from one of our newer members. He says we have a foreign believer visiting us today. Nelson, will you stand up." Nelson Lemming stood up. Harvey was getting nervous. "Nelson, will you bring this believer up here so we can greet him in the name of our Lord!"

Nelson grabbed Harvey's arm, and before Rev. Stilton knew what was happening, he was on his way to the altar of the Victory Bible Temple and Christian Family Life Center.

"Nelson, who do you have here?"

"Pastor Wayne, this here's Jacques LaGoom. He's from Belgium. His English ain't good."

Far above, Harvey could see his disguised image on one of the big screens. He hoped his beard and wig would stay in place. Rev. Cheapjack wrapped his arms around Harvey and squeezed. "God loves you, brother. I love you too."

Harvey could feel the right side of his fake beard coming loose.

With once great robotic voice the audience followed, "God loves you, brother. We love you too." Thousands stood and cheered.

Rev. Stilton smiled and waved, all the while praying that this was not being broadcast on one of those streaming channels.

"I know you don't understand me brother, but I just have to tell you and our world-wide television audience that Christians all over Hooperton and the world are coming to our Victory Bible Temple to hear the word of God. They are leaving those dead churches to feed from the trough of our prophetic ministry."

When the service resumed, instead of returning to his seat, Harvey slipped out a back door and ran all the way to his car, dropping his beard somewhere on the sidewalk. He got into his Checker and drove home quickly.

"My God, my God," he repeated over and over. "I had no idea the power people feel in that place. It's no wonder folks are flocking there."

Wednesday morning found the Rev. Stilton alone in his office.

"I may as well get to work on the sermon," Harvey said with resignation. He put away his lectionary text calculations, got up from his desk, and shuffled to the Roto-Sermon machine. Emotionless, he grabbed the lever and pulled. The great cogged wheels turned and arranged the cards into a sermon. He didn't like what he saw. He pulled the lever again creating another sermon.

"No, this isn't it. One more time."

He reached out and pulled. Yet another sermon was lined up. Harvey read the cards. He stepped back, looked at his great machine and let out a deep breath.

"This is ridiculous!" he thought. "No wonder everyone's leaving my church. Who in their right mind would ever listen to one of my sermons?"

Then, in the twinkling of an eye, the value Harvey had ascribed to his invention vanished. He remembered something Jesus had said: "For where your treasure is, there your heart will be also."

"This machine has drained me of every drop of inspiration I ever had," Harvey thought, shaking his head. "I've nothing in my heart that anyone would care to hear."

Feeling useless, directionless, and even a little angry, he put on his coat, said good-bye to Madeline Rottweiler, and went out for a long walk.

Harvey Stilton took a route that circled all of Hooperton. Guernsey McCudd passed him both on her way to the Hooperton Outlet Mall and on her way to the dentist later that morning. From his tractor Angus himself saw Harvey, and Sterling Hogg watched Harvey pass the bank. A disturbing thought kept coming back to Harvey: "I've treasured order, not my message, and along the way I've lost everything!"

After several hours he walked through a deserted part of town and passed an old decaying billboard. He stopped to look at it. Through all the grime and peeling paper, he could detect the image of a box of candied popcorn and peanuts. Looking closer he saw some writing. It said, "Free prize inside."

Right then and there, standing in front of that old dirty billboard, Harvey found his message. Perhaps it had always been there, deep in his heart. Nevertheless, he knew it was very, very, important.

"I need to get to work on my sermon right away!" he said to a stray dog that had wandered up to him. He had some excitement in his voice.

Rev. Stilton hurried back to his study at First Presbyterian Church of Hooperton. Abandoning his Roto-Sermon Machine, he got to work on the most important sermon of his life.

On Sunday morning Angus, Guernsey, Holstina, Ed, Sterling, Madeline, and the remnant of the First Presbyterian Church of Hooperton all noticed something very different about the Rev. Stilton. He was standing in the wooden pulpit, straight and tall with his head held high. Usually, Harvey slouched a little and leaned on his elbow.

Harvey opened his Bible and with great gentleness and sensitivity, he read a text from Galatians: "The fruit of the Spirit is love, joy, peace, patience, kindness, generosity, faithfulness, gentleness, and self-control. There is no law against such things."

Harvey looked up and smiled at the congregation. "You know that a lot of members have left our church these past months." Speaking more sternly, he continued, "And I think you all know where they've gone and why they have gone."

Harvey paused for a moment before saying what was really on his mind. "I've got a confession to make to you." Now the sanctuary was utterly silent, not whisper, not a cough nor even the slightest sniffle could be heard. "I have let you down," he said contritely. "For years I've not done right by you in my role as a preacher and teacher. And now, a lot of our brothers and sisters have had to go somewhere else to get their spiritual sustenance. I am truly sorry, but from now on things are going to change!" he said resolutely.

Every ear in the church was now fixed on Rev. Stilton for nobody wanted to miss what he had to say.

"There's something else," Harvey continued. "It saddens me to have to do it, but I'm going to be blunt. Hiding within the charisma of a great speaker is a gospel that's twisted. Some would have you believe that by obeying the Ten Commandments, or the Bible for that matter, you can earn God's favor. But that's not what St. Paul said!" Harvey made a fist and hit the lectern, but not too hard. The handful of people in the front pews noticed that his face was getting a little red. Yet Rev. Stilton had even more to say: "Paul said the good news of Jesus is all about a transformation of the heart." Harvey patted his chest as he spoke. He continued, "The Fruits of the Spirit the Apostle wrote about come out of this transformation. This is where we should focus our attention!" Harvey put his hands on his hips and stopped long enough to look at every face in the sanctuary (which wasn't very long).

"Do you remember that rectangular box of candied popcorn and peanuts you'd get when you were a kid? And do you remember what was so special about it? That prize buried deep inside." Harvey paused again and then leaned forward. "That's what these Fruits of the Spirit are," he said with enthusiasm, something the folks at First Presbyterian had not seen in their pastor before. "As we nurture our faith, they grow deep inside of us like peaches on the tree. They are the prize inside each of us, and they come from this transformation."

The sanctuary was perfectly still and quiet. There was no sound to be heard: not a whisper, or a snore, or the scratch of a pencil, not even a cell phone.

"And there is one more thing," Harvey said. "I think that when people feel love, joy, peace, patience, and all the other fruits from us, they just might want to be a part of our church. And maybe they will want to experience this transformation for themselves!"

Looking out over the sparsely populated sanctuary, Rev. Stilton departed from his text. "Come to think of it, there is something else I'd like to say. Do you remember who Jesus dined with? People the religious leaders called sinners and tax collectors. That's one of the reasons they hated Jesus. And do you know who should fill the pews of this sanctuary?" Harvey pointed all around. "The same kind of people—anyone who can't follow the Ten Commandments!" With that Harvey stepped out of the pulpit and sat down in his old rickety chair next to the choir loft.

The congregation was stunned. No one knew what to say or to do. So, they did what any good Presbyterian would do. They sat in their pews and waited for directions. Suddenly, Guernsey McCudd stood up and raised her arms in the air, accidentally bopping the back of Ed's head in the process. She hollered, "Amen!"

The following Sunday Harvey noticed a few new people in the congregation, people he had not seen before. Holstina had brought her new-age yoga instructor. Guernsey and Angus had convinced their secular-humanist-organic-farming friends to come as well. And sitting with Sterling Hogg was the one person Harvey thought the banker hated most: Karl Marx McEngels the last surviving member of the Hooperton Brotherhood of Atheistic and Socialistic Workers.

"I just wanted him to hear what you had to say," Sterling told Harvey after the service.

"Thank you, Sterling," Rev. Stilton said. "But I think he'll stick around because of you and everyone else."

"And I'll bet he hasn't a dime to pledge," Sterling laughed, poking fun at himself.

Angus came up to Harvey and remarked, "You got yourself a mighty message, Reverend. Your delivery could use improvin' some, but that message sure's good."

"Thank you, Angus," he replied. "I'll take that as a compliment."

Six months later, most of the members who left for Jimmy Splatterdash and his Victory Bible Temple and Christian Family Life Center had not returned to the First Presbyterian Church of Hooperton. Yet Harvey was still pleased because the new people coming were mostly folks who had not been to church before, who never gave Christianity or Jesus much thought at all. Rev. Stilton still was not a great preacher, no, not by a long shot. But on most Sundays Harvey did, in fact, have something very important to say. And these new folks continued to come, mostly because they wanted to be a part of the First Presbyterian Church community.

You might be wondering what Rev. Stilton did with his Roto-Sermon machine. It is still at First Presbyterian Church of Hooperton. The preacher moved it downstairs to the church kitchen where it is now used by the Hospitality Committee. The machine's vast sorting capabilities create a multitude of menu options for the Wednesday night fellowship suppers.

Pepi Pescado, chair of the Wednesday Evening Supper Sub-committee, was excited about the creativity and inspiration their new acquisition brought to his group. "Now-a we'll never serve-a the same 'carte du jour' twice-a, never!" he announced at the worship service one Sunday morning.

"This-a machine we have, she's-a truly amazing. Just-a wait till you-a see what-a-we gonna put in your tummy!"

With her story finished, Sue Moyers took a bow and sat down next to Jim and Ron.

"Sue, you give us Presbyterians hope," May Presley chuckled.

"There's your problem," Ron said. "You've got too much order."

"Search the Spirit!" Sue said. "Find God's message within you before you start organizing everything."

Ed Steale nodded his head. "I couldn't agree more."

"And remember, some of you need to go easy on that theological stuff." Rev. Boyle signaled agreement.

"Scares people," Ed said.

"Folks don't go to church to be educated," Ben added. "They want to worship the Lord, and they want strong moral values!"

"You think that'll get folks in our churches?" Rev. Moyers asked.

"They're coming our way for a reason," Billy replied. Ben and Bob nodded.

"Besides, you Methodists only make folks feel good, we give 'em the morals stuff, too," Ben Boyle interjected. "That's why they flock to my church.

"But isn't it love that should attract the masses?" Jim Mayer suggested.

"You're absolutely right "Ron said. "Paul did say, 'God loves those who love themselves.'"

"Paul?" Princeton asked incredulously. "Paul never said anything like that."

"Sure, he did," Ron said.

"Try Ben Franklin," offered Dave.

"Ben Franklin?"

"Yeah, and I think he said something like 'God helps those who help themselves.'"

"But Ron and Jim still have a point," Sue said. "It's always been God's love that draws people to church!"

"But, sometimes you gotta scare them!" Ed added.

"Enough! It's time to hear from us Presbyterians!" May Presley stood up and headed for the front of the bus. Everyone turned around and looked at May with great expectations. "My tale is about a Methodist church up yonder in Atlanta." She opened a bent and dog-eared pocket New Testament her mother had given her long ago. "My scripture comes from Matthew eighteen, three, to be exact: 'Unless you become like children, you will never enter the kingdom,' our Lord declares." She closed her Bible and continued, "My esteemed Irreverents," she chuckled, poking fun at everyone. "I call my tale, 'The Church in the Sky.'"

The Church in the Sky

Truly I tell you, unless you change and become like children, you will never enter the kingdom of heaven.

(Matthew 18:3 NRSV)

"Sputnik! Come back here. At once!" J. Roderick yelled.

Sputnik, a single-minded, nine-pound miniature terrier with a coat like steel wool was chasing after a terrorized delivery clerk from Atlanta's Gentility Catering. The clerk, Bill Wiley, a college sophomore, worked weekends for the catering service and disliked Sputnik. Sputnik disliked anyone who made deliveries. At full throttle Bill, with Sputnik at his heels, turned the corner and headed down the long hallway that led to a private elevator. The oriental carpet runner gave the dog added traction and helped him gain ground. Yet Bill managed to slip into the elevator just as the doors were closing, almost catching the dog's nose in the process.

"Sputnik, get away from that elevator, immediately!" J. Roderick Westmoreland made it to the hallway but had to stop. His eighty-five-year-old legs could go no further. Sputnik barked, growled, and yapped at the closed doors until he had had his say. "Little dog, we are attempting to prepare for church. I must say, you are not helping in the least." Sputnik, his head held high and his tail erect, turned away from the elevator, walked past Mr. Westmoreland, and headed back towards the condominium's kitchen. Mr. Westmoreland shook his head and followed Sputnik down the hallway.

Inside the kitchen, members of the Middle Buckhead Methodist Chapel were readying the brunch they would enjoy following their Sunday morning service. Ninety-five-year-old Catherine Summerville was carefully transferring the delicate crab soufflé, the finger quiches, and the poached quail eggs which Bill Wiley had just delivered, onto the church's sterling silver serving trays. Over in the butler's pantry, octogenarians Katerina Battenberg and Elizabeth Buchanan were gathering plates and glasses from a collection of eighteenth century Wedgewood china and stemware from an equally old set of Irish crystal. In the adjoining room, William Ridgecrest, himself a centenarian, was choosing several sonatas from an extensive music collection that consisted entirely of sheet music, some of it quite old. They didn't own any recorded music. William, Katerina, and Catherine made sizable contributions to the symphony and had come to appreciate that personal touch afforded by the private concerts they received in return. Three violins, a viola, a cello, two flutes and several woodwinds were due at 1:00 pm. sharp.

As far as Protestant congregations go, Middle Buckhead Methodist Chapel is atypical. What makes it unusual, though, is neither its limitless financial liquidity nor the distinguished bloodlines of some of its members. No, it is the astonishing fact that Middle Buckhead Methodist Chapel has been lost. Aside from the members themselves, there is not one single minister, lay-person, district superintendent, or bishop (retired or active) who has any recollection or record of its existence. Even more incredibly, the members of Middle Buckhead Methodist Chapel have no clue that this has happened to them.

So how exactly do you lose an entire congregation—people, building, grounds, and everything else? And how is it that the folks who pay the bills and who come to worship Sunday after Sunday are in the dark, so to speak? In the case of Middle Buckhead Methodist Chapel, it was the combined effect of five remarkable events that all happened on one fate-filled Tuesday over sixty years ago.

On September 17, 1957, at 6:30 in the morning, conference Bishop Lamar Binghamton was killed in a horrific accident involving seven cars, a dump truck, and a blimp. A half hour later, an electrical malfunction in a toaster that sat in the bishop's conference center offices started a fire that burned the kitchen as well as the office of the Rev. Bo Cusped, upon whose desk sat the complete records of the Middle Buckhead Methodist Chapel. The church had applied for permission to move the choir loft from the back of the altar to parallel rows on each side. Bo had pulled the church's files the night before and left them on his desk to be reviewed. Amazingly, at 7:23 a.m., a pipe in the ceiling at city hall had burst. For a full ninety minutes, water gushed onto a table upon which sat the real estate records of this same church. Attorney Clayton A. Roswell had left them out the previous afternoon, intending to return in the morning to complete the renovation permit applications. The emergency repair crew had saved nothing. Then, at 8:30 a.m., the following transatlantic cable was sent from Spain to the Middle Buckhead Methodist Chapel and to the bishop's conference center office:

Fr Rev J Walker Stop
In Love W/ Olive Heiress Stop
Not Coming Back Ever Stop

The congregation's vacationing pastor, Rev. Jim Walker, had fallen madly in love with an Andalusian heiress and would never return to the United States. Because of the early morning fire, this cable was never delivered to the bishop. Finally, at 9:00 a.m., Mr. Roswell and the Rev. Cusped were both arrested by Fulton County police officers and quickly extradited to Arkansas where they were to face felony charges for mail fraud. Later that evening, at 9:53, the small plane taking them to the town of Hasty crashed in a remote area of the Ozarks, leaving no survivors. And thus, vanished Middle Buckhead Methodist Chapel, bureaucratically speaking.

Unaware of their disappearance, the parishioners vainly waited six decades both for a reply to their renovation application and for the bishop to assign a new preacher. This incredible wait came not from a wellspring of forbearance. Quite the contrary, parishioners had no patience with the folks at the conference center and believed they were all a bunch of lazy, paper-pushing bureaucrats.

"You know, they'll never get their act together," Mr. Westmoreland said back in sixty-three. "A dilly-dallying ecclesiastical hierarchy, that's what they are!"

During the height of President Ford's administration, Ms. Summerville suggested they send a representative downtown to see the bishop and find out what was taking so long. However, in a nearly unanimous vote at the congregation's charge conference meeting, this idea was tabled.

"I don't believe it would do any good," Mr. Ridgecrest had said at the time, summing up the skepticism of almost everyone. "If they knew what they were doing, they would have sent us a new preacher and approved our choir loft long ago."

For six decades the members made do with what they had. Several members were pretty good at public speaking, and so they shared the duties of reading passages from the Bible and giving short speeches from the pulpit, often patriotic in nature. Communion was dispensed with altogether without a single complaint, for it had always made the Sunday service go on much too long. Given the age of the congregation, requests for baptisms and weddings simply never arose. And as far as pastoral counseling was concerned, most members of Middle Buckhead Methodist Chapel didn't approve of it anyway.

"Personal problems need to remain just that," Elizabeth Buchanan said the last time the topic arose.

Though a new preacher never came, the choir loft was finally moved during Thanksgiving weekend in 1979. It wasn't, however, set into parallel aisles as originally planned. Instead, the swinging steel ball from a wrecking crane transformed the old wooden choir pews as well as the whole church into a heap of bricks, glass, and splintered wood. Middle Buckhead Methodist chapel was sold to developer A.J. Strongarm who converted the property into a mixed-use retail/office complex. The remaining members took the proceeds from the sale and purchased the top floor of a thirty-five story Peachtree Street condominium, which they then converted into the new home for their congregation. The parish council had voted to go ahead with the condominium project after mailing three notifications to the conference office and bishop, all of which went unanswered. They did not know that the conference offices had moved in 1969 and that their letters were being delivered to an abandoned building.

J. Roderick Westmoreland, Catherine Summerville, Katerina Battenberg, Elizabeth Buchanan, and William Ridgecrest, who formed the remnant of Middle Buckhead Methodist Chapel, and seven other members who had since "gone on ahead," chose the new location for several reasons, the chief of which was to be closer to God and to be further from the enclosing urban chaos. Not only did they buy the top floor, individually they each purchased residences on the ones below. These last surviving members, known internally as "The Five," had not set foot outside of the thirty-five-story condominium building since the day they all moved in.

The penthouse sanctuary needed only a few improvements before it was ready for services. This time however, the members were not going to bother asking for permission from the conference center. In the living room they installed cushioned mahogany prayer recliners in front of a bank of windows that overlooked Atlanta. Here, up in the sky, they could relax and pray for the denizens scurrying below, never having to become involved with the messiness of life in a major metropolitan area. Also, the original architects and contractors had modified the private elevator so that, in addition to stopping at the lobby and parking level, it would also stop on those floors where the members themselves now lived.

Elizabeth perfectly described this arrangement of living and worshiping in the same building when she said, "It's just like having our own luxury high-rise monastery."

J. Roderick Westmoreland was the newest member of Middle Buckhead Methodist Chapel, assuming of course, you don't count Sputnik. J. Roderick joined the congregation shortly after taking a post in the Atlanta office of the old War Department the week before D Day. He had transferred his membership from the John Wesley Methodist Church in Columbus, Georgia, a large congregation named after John Koker Wesley, the wealthy bottler of the now defunct beverage Koker Kola. Middle Buckhead's other remaining members were all lifetime attendees, the youngest being confirmed shortly before the first Model A Ford rolled off the old assembly line on Ponce de Leon Avenue. Sputnik arrived just three years ago. One winter Sunday morning he stepped off the private elevator as it arrived on the thirty-fifth floor and immediately behaved as though he had title to the property. No one knew from where he came, and so they let him stay.

With Sputnik back in the kitchen, J. Roderick Westmoreland could continue with the final touches of his Sunday talk. This week was his turn to read a Bible passage and to give a little speech. Within five minutes the text was finished. He then went into the living room and placed the hymnals, Bibles, and handwritten bulletins on the pews salvaged from their old church building.

"I'm ready when you are," he called, summoning the others.

The four gradually made their way into the living room to take their seats.

J. Roderick stepped to the lectern, opened his large-print, black-leather Bible, and read a selection from Revelation: "And the shape of the locusts were like unto horses prepared unto battle." J. Roderick loved the Bible's great battle chapters and would add a lot of drama to his readings. He continued, "And they had tails like unto scorpions, and there were stings in their tails: and their power was to hurt men five months." With both arms swinging, he did his best to simulate a flying scorpion.

"I bet we're going to hear his War Department stories today," Catherine whispered to Elizabeth, who started giggling.

"He's going to tell us about the time he picked up Secretary Stimson at the airport," Elizabeth suggested, still snickering.

After closing his Bible, J. Roderick looked to the tattered forty-eight-star flag he kept as a war souvenir. It hung on a wall in the room. A small tear ran down his cheek. "It seems like yesterday, December 14, 1944, a day that will live in my memory. War Department Secretary Henry Stimson arrived in secret at Atlanta's army airfield in a great B-24 Liberator. I alone had the honor of serving as his driver."

Elizabeth leaned over to Catherine, "Do you think he'll talk about the gold service pin Mr. Stimson gave him?"

J. Roderick reached into his pocket and pulled out a small worn leather box. He opened it and held it up for all to see.

"This pin was given to me by Secretary Stimson when the war was over. I did not deserve it. I wasn't with our boys on the beaches at Normandy, nor was I with them when they reached Guadalcanal. I couldn't go. But I did my best to serve my country."

"Now he's going to tell us how disorderly young people are today," Catherine whispered. J. Roderick put the box back in his pocket. "Young people today don't love their country like we did. They are not disciplined. This country has no order now, and children are not properly managed. But thanks be to God, now we have this safe abode, high above that higgledy-piggledy world."

The others did indeed find Mr. Westmoreland's Sunday talk pretty inspiring though its power diminished a bit each time they heard it. Then, accompanied by Catherine Summerville on the Steinway, the congregation sang a few of their most cherished hymns, including "Come Ye Sinners Poor and Needy," "Come Let Us Join Our Friends Above," and J. Roderick's favorite, "Am I a Soldier of the Cross?" Following the hymns they sat in the recliners while Katerina Battenberg led them in petitions for their health, for the city and the citizens below, for the nation, and for the governor and president, though they had lost track of who these leaders were.

"I believe we can enjoy our brunch now. The symphony members should be along presently," Elizabeth Buchanan announced.

The Five helped each other up from their seats, and together they headed into the kitchen. Sputnik was already there waiting for scraps and spills when the sound of the private elevator reaching the thirty-fifth floor triggered the dog's internal alarm. Sputnik popped up in the air, spun a full one hundred and eighty degrees and sped towards the elevator door.

"Sputnik causes me such consternation!" an irritated Mr. Westmoreland said as he put his food down and hurried after the dog. "A modicum of discipline, that's all I ask," he muttered under his breath.

Sputnik was already heading down the hallway just as the crowded elevator full of symphony members and musical instruments arrived at the thirty-fifth floor.

"Sputnik! Come back here!" Mr. Westmoreland yelled.

The doors of the elevator opened, spilling the musicians and their precious instruments into the hallway. At warp speed, Sputnik had already passed the carpet runner and was sliding on the polished marble floors in a direct collision course with Antonio Frobolli's seventeenth century Viennese cello. The panicked cellist raised his priceless instrument into the air, and Sputnik slid underneath, straight into the elevator just as the doors were closing.

Fortune's wheel was turning fast that day: Bill Wiley was on the ground floor waiting for the same private elevator. He had forgotten to deliver one of the quail egg servings and wanted to drop the item off before going home. Bill's summoning of the elevator brought Sputnik down to the lobby.

Having spent the last three years doing "his business" on the grassy penthouse terrace, Sputnik had never experienced dropping thirty-five floors. By the time the doors opened, the little dog was in a state of panic. Like a rocket, Sputnik shot out of the elevator, knocking the startled delivery clerk onto the floor. The dog then sped through the lobby at the same time that a delivery man from the Furniture Depot had propped open the front door. Sputnik saw the opening and darted outside onto Peachtree Street.

"Did you see the dog?" an anxious J. Roderick asked Bill Wiley as the delivery clerk got off the elevator.

"Man, he was flying. That dog knocked me on the floor and broke your eggs!"

"Where?" asked J. Roderick.

"I left them on the floor downstairs" a still-dazed Bill Wiley replied.

"Not the eggs, I mean my dog!"

"Oh, yeah. I think he ran outside," he said, rubbing the back of his head.

Hearing J. Roderick's excited voice, the other four worked their way from the kitchen to the elevator.

"Did the dog get out?" Elizabeth Buchanan asked nervously.

"Yes, and someone needs to go after him," J. Roderick replied.

"J. Roderick, you're the only one who doesn't need a cane," Catherine said.

"It's been twelve years since I've been down there," he protested. "You know what it's like now!"

"But you can't let our Sputnik get away. You must find him, quickly!"

A fearful J. Roderick Westmoreland walked to the elevator door, and with his hands shaking nervously, he pushed the call button. The elevator arrived, the door opened, and the old War Department veteran stepped in. He turned around to face his fellow parishioners and waved good-bye.

Exiting the elevator, J. Roderick walked across the lobby and asked the Furniture Depot workers about Sputnik. Yes, they did see him. One of them pointed down Peachtree Street, indicating the direction the dog had taken. J. Roderick closed his eyes, held his breath, and went outside. It was a bright spring day, and the sun was shining in a beautiful blue sky. Feeling the warmth on his skin, he opened his eyes and carefully walked down the driveway to a very busy Peachtree Street. There he could see Sputnik trotting along the sidewalk heading south towards downtown.

"Sputnik," J. Roderick yelled. "Come back, please!" But his voice could not be heard above the motors and horns of all the cars and trucks.

J. Roderick took another deep breath and started after Sputnik, but his old legs would carry him only so fast. Fortunately, the dog had stopped to peek through the glass doors of the Atlanta Pancake Shop, allowing Mr. Westmoreland time to catch up.

Sputnik looked up at J. Roderick and wagged his tail. "Let's go in," the dog seemed to plead.

"You're interested in this establishment?" J. Roderick Westmoreland asked with amazement. He had never taken a dog inside a restaurant before.

"In," seemed to be the reply.

"I guess we could go in for a little while, but we can't stay long. The others will worry about us." J. Roderick picked up the dog and opened the door.

Inside the pancake shop they took a seat in the nearest vacant booth. Sputnik tapped his front right paw on a picture of Canadian bacon on the cover of the menu. To press his point, the dog licked the picture.

"Hungry?" J. Roderick asked. When the server arrived, he requested a cup of coffee and an order of Canadian bacon.

Looking around the restaurant, J. Roderick noticed a young woman with a toddler who was enjoying a plate of pancakes, the majority of which was on the floor. The child looked at J. Roderick, smiled, and threw a handful of syrupy pancakes at him.

"Gosh, I'm so sorry, Mister," the mother said apologetically. "I took him to a Braves game last weekend, and ever since then I can't get him to stop throwing things. I hope he didn't get any on you."

Her comment pulled J. Roderick's thoughts away from the flying pancakes to a distant and dusty memory of his own father teaching him to throw a baseball. Strange as it might seem, it felt good to have a child throw food at him. "It's quite all right, madame," he said. "No harm done."

"Do you have any kids?" she asked, pulling several pieces of sticky pancake from her own long hair.

"They're grown," he answered. "They both live on the West Coast. One has children in college. You know, I haven't seen them in nearly ten years."

"That's kinda sad, mister," she said. "You must be lonely."

"No, I have my friends. I have my church. They keep me busy." He then thought to himself, "Has it been ten years since I've seen my boys? How did we get so disconnected?"

J. Roderick finished his coffee and Sputnik his Canadian bacon. They said good-bye to the woman and her child and left the restaurant.

Once outside, they headed north on Peachtree Street back towards their condominium building. About half-way there J. Roderick needed to rest his legs. He carried Sputnik to a wooden bench in a small street-side park and sat down. All around them were flowering dogwoods and azaleas, now in full bloom.

"My, I'd forgotten the beauty of an Atlanta springtime close-up."

He smiled at a little girl who was working on a pink bubble gum-flavored ice cream cone a yard or two away. She smiled back and wandered over to see Sputnik, who seemed to her a very strange-looking doggie. Reaching to pet him, she dropped her melting cone upside down in J. Roderick's lap and then started crying.

Her older brother was already running towards them. "Oh gosh, I'm so sorry, mister. I was supposed to be watching her. She's made a huge mess on your pants."

J. Roderick's white linen trousers now had a very large, round, pink spot. The first thought that entered his mind, however, was another memory of his father. This time he was on the back stoop of his childhood home watching him turn the crank of an old wooden, hand-operated ice cream maker. "I'll bet I haven't had ice cream in twenty years," J. Roderick thought.

Sputnik barked, and with his nose seemed to be pointing at the girl's cone, which was now resting upside down next to J. Roderick's shoe. "I want ice cream," he seemed to be communicating.

"I'll get us all some ice cream!" cried J. Roderick.

He found the vendor and bought four cones: vanilla for the boy, bubblegum for the little girl, chocolate for himself, and for Sputnik, rocky road.

"Young man, you have a lovely sister there," J. Roderick said. "She didn't mean to ruin my pants. I'm fine, believe me." Mr. Westmoreland looked at his watch. "And we'd better get back to the church," he said to Sputnik. "They must be worried by now."

It took Sputnik and J. Roderick about twenty minutes to reach their Peachtree Street condominium building, and all along the way they marveled at the countless blooming flowers, butterflies, and the occasional hummingbird. Before entering the building, they turned around to take one last long look.

"I can't believe how much I've missed all these years. God's creation is so beautiful," he said to Sputnik.

They walked through the lobby and got into the private elevator as quickly as they could. The doors closed behind them, and J. Roderick and Sputnik began their ascent to the thirty-fifth floor.

Back in the kitchen with Sputnik at his side, a weary J. Roderick told the others all about the glorious flowers, eating ice cream with two children and, looking down at Sputnik, the pancake shop.

"He's getting loopy," Katerina commented. "Now what is that on your shirt?" she asked.

"Syrup."

"And your pants, what in heaven's name is that?"

"That's bubblegum ice cream."

"J. Roderick, are you growing a mustache?"

He wiped his mouth with his starched handkerchief and chuckled, "That's chocolate."

"He's loopy, all right," Katerina repeated.

William leaned over to smell his breath. "Have you been into the schnapps?"

"Look, I'm fine. But I am going back down there."

"J. Roderick Westmoreland, you can't! You must stay up here. It's dangerous down there. Just like you said this morning!"

"I'm going back, and all of you are coming too!"

William, Catherine, Elizabeth, and Katerina did their best to convince J. Roderick to abandon his foolishness, but the old War Department veteran would not bend.

"Well, it is a pretty day," Catherine said, feeling tempted. After several minutes of discussion, she suggested they "only take a careful step or two outside the front door."

"I guess that wouldn't be so dangerous," Elizabeth agreed.

The Five got into the elevator and for the first time in twelve years, descended together to the ground floor.

"Hope the cables hold," William grumbled. The others whimpered.

"We'll be fine," J. Roderick said calmly.

Wagging his tail, an excited Sputnik looked up at J. Roderick. "Oh, boy! Outside! Again!"

Arriving at ground level, they exited the elevator, and with J. Roderick in the lead and Sputnik as caboose, they headed across the lobby in single file. Bright sunlight was streaming through the glass lobby doors. Outside they could see the display of flowers and green plants that lined the condominium's driveway.

"I'd forgotten what it was like down here," Elizabeth said.

J. Roderick stopped at the front door and turned to the others. Their faces spoke of their trepidation.

"I want to go back up," Katerina cried.

J. Roderick took her by the hand and, with great gentleness, led her outside. Through the windows the others could see her look up to the sky and point with her cane. "Birds!" Catherine thought Katerina had said. Mr. Westmoreland came back inside, put his arm around Catherine, and carefully helped her out the front door. Next was Elizabeth. When he came in for William, the centenarian was crying. Arm-in-arm they went outside. Finally, J. Roderick came back in for Sputnik who was wagging his tail so furiously he couldn't keep his back legs still.

"We're going outside again!" he said to the dog.

In single file the Five plus one dog walked along the driveway sidewalk towards Peachtree Street. They looked at the flowers, touched the leaves within reach, and laughed at the flock of birds overhead. To passers-by they seemed like children going outside for the first time.

William grabbed J. Roderick by the arm. "I want one of those pink ice cream cones."

"It's so wonderful," Catherine marveled.

By now every member of Middle Buckhead Methodist Chapel was feeling quite brave and frisky. Then a city bus stopped in front of their building, letting off several of the people who worked in their condominium.

Catherine looked back at J. Roderick, "Let's get on!" she yelled.

Sputnik sped to the bus and jumped in without touching a single step. One by one, J. Roderick helped the others in before climbing on board himself. The Five took their seats along one side of the bus.

"Where's this thing going?" William asked the driver.

"This is the J-9 bus, Sir," the driver replied. "Grant Park and the zoo."

The bus started out onto Peachtree Street, merged into the fast-paced city traffic, and continued its circuitous route to the zoo.

"I'm so excited," shrieked Elizabeth. "I haven't been to a zoo in ages."

"You folks must be new to this city," the driver said.

Sputnik and the other four looked at J. Roderick, who paused for a moment before responding.

"You know, I guess you could say that. Yes, we are new to this city," he said.

Out of the back window they could see their building fade into the distance, and through the front and side windows images of the city, good and bad, passed by them.

William was laughing. "I feel like a kid again!"

"Sputnik, come back here!" J. Roderick said sternly.

The dog had darted to the front of the bus and was now seated atop the dashboard, looking through the windshield.

"He's okay, Mister," the driver said. "He's just itching to go somewhere."

Sputnik looked at J. Roderick and barked.

"It's time for all of us to go somewhere," J. Roderick told the driver. "We've been in the sky for a long time."

"Y'all flew down for some kinda conference or something?"

"We flew down, that's true," J. Roderick replied with a chuckle.

"For whom are all those people waiting?" Elizabeth asked the driver, pointing to a long line that stretched for nearly two city blocks. "Goodness me, I don't like the looks of that crowd," she added. The bus was now passing a single-story, ramshackle brick building that, back in the twenties, was home to a dry goods wholesaler.

"Not for whom, for what," the driver replied. "They're hungry. That's some kind of soup kitchen. I think it's run by the Methodists."

"We're Methodists," William said. "And I don't think they'd go for something like that."

"Not the Methodists we know," Katerina added.

The bus pulled to the curb and stopped for passengers. Sputnik darted out the door.

Several months later, Sputnik was again after Bill Wiley of Gentility Catering, nipping at his heels. Bill had just finished delivering Sunday brunch.

"Sputnik! Sputnik! Not the elevator again!" J. Roderick yelled.

Unfortunately for Bill, the large cart he had to use, now that the Sunday crowd at Middle Buckhead Methodist Chapel had burgeoned to nearly one hundred men, women, and children slowed his hasty retreat to the elevator.

"They don't pay me enough," he grumbled.

"Don't you get on that elevator, Sputnik!" J. Roderick ordered.

The dog stopped at the end of the hallway and yapped at Bill as he rolled the big cart onto the elevator.

This particular Sunday, Methodist Bishop Lamar Binghamton III, had joined the ninety-four very hungry folks who had recently become regular worshipers at Middle Buckhead, some even joining the congregation. Most of these folks were poor; some were lame; and a few were even blind. When Bill Wiley arrived, they were all in the condominium sanctuary singing the last hymn for the morning, "Come Let Us Join Our Friends Above." They would soon enjoy a sumptuous meal of roast duck with Belgian endives, whipped garlic-rosemary potatoes, and Alsatian green beans with almonds slivers. Afterwards, woodwinds from the Atlanta Symphony were scheduled to play.

When Katerina, Elizabeth, Catherine, William and J. Roderick finished organizing the meal, the old War Department veteran stood at the sanctuary doorway and called everyone to the table.

"Come, for our feast is ready," J. Roderick bellowed, his voice filled with new-found joy. Sputnik, now weighing in at twelve pounds, was standing next to him, excited over the sudden bonanza of table scraps from this growing congregation.

"You folks are wonderful," Bishop Binghamton said to Mr. Westmoreland. "You've shared everything you have with these people." He put his arm around J. Roderick and patted him on the back. "Only a month ago I had no idea you people were here, and those folks, well, they were in line at a dismal soup kitchen."

"Thank you, Bishop, but I don't think we're that wonderful."

"What do you mean? Look around at these people," the bishop said. "You've been a real blessing to them. We're proud of you!"

"I've spent a lifetime barricading myself," J. Roderick said quietly, with a little sadness in his voice. "I've barely begun dismantling this fortress in which I live. No, I am not a real blessing."

"We owe everything to public transportation," Elizabeth said, cutting in. She had been listening to their conversation.

Then Catherine joined in. "That's the only way to see the world," she said.

"I still don't understand," Bishop Binghamton said. "Quit talking to me in parables."

"We were heading to the zoo, on a whim," William explained. He too had been listening to Bishop Binghamton and J. Roderick. "But we had to stop and meet these people."

"It's Sputnik's fault. He nearly got away when he jumped out of our bus," Katerina added. She also had been listening. "And we never made it to the zoo."

Lamar shook his head in confusion. "You people don't make any sense to me."

"One day," J. Roderick said. "Perhaps one day we will."

Before Mr. Westmoreland could say another word, Sputnik jumped to his feet and sped to the elevator door, barking and yapping all the way there. The Atlanta Symphony woodwinds had arrived.

"I'll be right back," J. Roderick said to the bishop. "I must attend to that dog, forthwith."

"May, I am impressed," Sarah Priestly said. "There's something in it for each one of us to take home."

"That's for sure," Rev. Ben Boyle said. "Especially for the Methodists! You're sinking under all that bureaucracy."

"Sure, can't call you guys down-to-earth," Ed laughed.

"Now you wait a minute," Rev. Jim Mayer protested angrily "That's not true at all. The Buckhead church members found their mission just like Harvey Stilton!"

"But if they had been like us," Bob said. "It wouldn't have taken so long!" Ben and Bill nodded in agreement.

"Same with me!" Ed Steale added. "God gives me a mission; I go do it. I don't need anybody asking me, 'Who moved my choir loft?'"

Wanting to stay out of the fray, Ken Lesley remained quiet. He was thinking about his irritating choir director who kept rearranging everything.

"We non-doms can do anything we want to," Ed added. "No higher-ups to stop us from doing God's will!"

"And look at the nitwits that end up in your pulpits!" Princeton Newport said. "Remember the felon at that Augusta Bible temple? How much did he steal?"

"If I got the story right, that guy was wanted in Mississippi and Alabama, too!" Jim added laughing.

"It had nothin' to do with me!"

"Didn't he preach at your revival?"

"Enough!" Rev. Tucker cut in. "Who's next? Please continue, I pray!"

"I'm next," Rev. Billy Barker said, standing up. "And I have a tale about the family—something that's important to each and every one of us on this bus."

"Amen," Ben and Bob added for emphasis. "The family is number one for us Baptists."

"Oh great, it's family-values time." Sarah shook her head.

"Stop the bus! Get me out of here!" Sue Moyers called.

"What is it with you people?" Billy asked. "Every time we bring up the family, you people flee."

"What have you against the family?" Ben asked, rhetorically.

"Oh, give me a break." May was getting angry.

"Look everybody, shush," Billy said, getting up from his seat and stepping to the front of the bus. "Let me tell my tale. Trust me, you'll like it. Luke is my source, from chapter twelve: 'Your treasure is where your heart is,' Jesus told us." Billy paused for a moment to gather his thoughts and then continued. "My story I call, 'The Night of Aunt Sheila's Visit.'"

The Night of Aunt Sheila's Visit

For where your treasure is, there your heart will be also.

(LUKE 12:34 NRSV)

"DID YOU GET THE mail, dear?" Lionel yelled from inside his home office.

"Yes, love. I've got it." His wife, Smyrna, was in the kitchen sorting through a stack of letters, bills, magazines, catalogues, and flyers. "Honey, we've been pre-approved again," she said sarcastically. "Another of those ubiquitous platinum cards." When she reached an envelope made from homemade paper, she froze. "Oh, here's Aunt Sheila's letter!"

"She's a bit late sending it this year, isn't she?" Lionel said, wandering into the kitchen.

"Oh, my gosh, what's today's date?"

"It's the fifth," Lionel replied. "Why?"

"This envelope was postmarked two months ago," Smyrna said, handing it to her husband. "Aunt Sheila will be here tonight. We've got to get the house ready!"

Lionel ran down to the basement. He located five large cardboard boxes, all of them labeled, "Aunt Sheila's Visits." One by one he lugged them upstairs to a frantic Smyrna. They opened the first box.

"You take the bathroom, I'll take the kids' room," Smyrna directed.

Lionel grabbed some of the contents and ran upstairs to the bathroom. He pulled the soap from the sink and bathtub, replacing it with Aunt

Sheila's lard soap. Likewise, he exchanged the shampoo and cream rinse for her concoction of potash, salt, and rinds. Lionel took the bath towels and washcloths, tossing them into the hamper. He replaced them with fleece towels and horsehair rags. The toothpaste went too. Lionel traded it for the paste Aunt Sheila made with the magnesium and phosphate she dug from a hillside on the old family homestead.

Smyrna was in the children's bedroom. Gone were the sheets, blankets, and comforters. She quickly remade the beds with homespun cotton sheets and the blankets that Aunt Sheila wove herself with hair shorn from her sheep. Smyrna took down the Taylor Swift, Billie Eilish, and Bad Bunny posters and replaced them with the portraits of Herschel, a prize-winning pig; Josephine, a record-setting dairy cow; and Wisenheimer the Weimaraner. She ran downstairs and grabbed another set of sheets, blankets, and portraits and headed to hers and Lionel's bedroom.

Five minutes later Lionel and Smyrna met back at the boxes. "You take the living room; I'll do the dining room," Smyrna said.

"Right!" Lionel took an armful of bronzed hoofs, county fair ribbons, pictures, doilies, and an Afghan made from crocheted mohair and darted down the hallway. Smyrna took an arrangement of dried corn stalks and flax and headed to the dining room.

"Honey, why do we do this every year?" Lionel asked his wife as the two slumped onto a couch, exhausted. "I wish I could toss those boxes!"

"Aside from the farm, we're all she has," Smyrna said with resignation. She looked at her husband. "She'd be devastated if she didn't feel needed. I think she just might give up altogether."

"But this is ridiculous."

"Mom, Dad, we're home!" Mary yelled.

Back from a baseball game, Mary slammed the door as she and her sister Annie entered the house.

"Can't you be gentler?" Smyrna pleaded.

"Sorry Mom."

"Girls, I need to tell you something. Aunt Sheila's coming tonight."

"What?" Mary cried.

"Tonight?" Annie screamed.

Lionel tried to calm his daughters, "Now girls, she'll be here for only a couple of days."

"But Dad!"

The girls' objections were suddenly drowned by a noisy diesel engine outside. Lionel, Smyrna, Mary, and Annie ran to the window. An old mud-encrusted, smoke-spewing flatbed truck riddled with dings and dents was pulling into the driveway.

"This is mortifying!" Annie cried. "What will everyone think?"

Attached to the truck was a house-trailer made of corrugated metal and plywood.

"Oh, dear," Lionel muttered. "There goes my lawn."

On the back of the flatbed truck, tied to the wooden fence sides, stood Herschel, Josephine, and Wisenheimer the Weimaraner.

"Yoo-hoo!" Aunt Sheila untied the driver's door and climbed out of the truck. "Yoo-hoo! Smyrna! Children! Lyle! Yoo-hoo!"

"Please, everybody," Smyrna begged. "Smile!"

Smyrna opened the front door and stepped outside onto the stoop. "Aunt Sheila! We're so glad you're here!" Lionel, Mary, and Annie stood behind Smyrna waving.

Annie whispered to Mary, "I wish we were waving good-bye."

First Smyrna and then Lionel hugged Aunt Sheila when she got to the front door.

"I see you brought the gang, again," Lionel said, forcing a smile.

"They so hate being alone." Pointing to her trailer, Aunt Sheila said, "Lyle, I have some boxes for everyone. Would you and the kids be so kind as to get them for me?"

Smyrna took Aunt Sheila by the hand and led her inside. "His name is Lionel, not Lyle," she said gently.

"Oh, I'm sorry. He's so picky about his name, isn't he?"

"You're welcome to sleep in the house," Smyrna said. "You can use the guest room." The family was at the dining room table. Wisenheimer, lying in a pile of his shedding hair and tracked-in dirt and mud, was asleep on the floor, and Herschel and Josephine were in the backyard looking at everyone through a breath-fogged, nose-streaked sliding-glass door.

"I don't want to be a burden. You just pretend I'm not here." Aunt Sheila handed Annie her large casserole dish filled to the brim with a mixture of kale, collard greens, and chard. "Here, child. Take as much as you like. There's plenty more in the trailer." To Mary she passed a container stuffed with scrapple. "Daddy loved this stuff; eat up. It's an old family recipe. And you need the fat."

Mary and Annie looked to their mother. Their mouths silently formed the word, "help."

"Now Aunt Sheila, you know teenagers are picky eaters," Smyrna said, trying to come to their rescue. "Don't be upset if they won't eat much."

"It's okay, dear. They'll love my grainy gruel in the morning." Speaking to her nieces, she said, "Children, after breakfast I'll show you how to make slop with the leftovers. Herschel loves it." She turned to Lionel, "Lyle, we need to collect Josephine's manure when we get up. It's for fuel and I'm sure you'll wanna dry some of it for your grill."

"Bye, Aunt Sheila, bye!" Smyrna, Lionel, Mary, and Annie were on the front stoop collectively shouting their farewells above the noise of the old diesel truck. The five days that seemed so long and arduous had come to an end.

"See you next year!" Annie yelled. "Thanks for the mohair!"

Mary jumped in, "Thank you Aunt Sheila. I love the straw jacket!"

"Thank Josephine for the grill fuel," Lionel added. Smyrna elbowed him.

"Tootle-oo!" Aunt Sheila was waving at the family through the windshield as she was backing out of the driveway. Fortunately for a neighbor driving down the street (and for his insurance company as well), she suddenly stopped and stuck her head out the window. "Tootle-oo-love-you-I-do! I hope I'll be back next year!" Aunt Sheila yelled. "I can't wait," Lionel muttered sarcastically. Smyrna elbowed him again.

Herschel, Josephine, and Wisenheimer were on the back of the flatbed, tied to the wooden fences and looking through the slats. The pig and cow were happy to be heading back to their paddock and pasture, far away from the confines of suburbia. Once on the street, Sheila hit the accelerator and disappeared into a cloud of exhaust, dirt, and bits of hay.

Lionel let out a long sigh. "Whew." He put his arm around Smyrna. "Now we can get back to normal."

"I'm taking a bath with real soap!" Mary said. She ran into the house; Annie followed close behind.

"You know, I feel sorry for her," Smyrna said to her husband. "She tries so hard to please us."

"You're right, dear. I should be more patient and understanding." Lionel and Smyrna walked back into the house. "I just wish she wouldn't call me Lyle."

"At least it's only once a year."

Ten months later, Smyrna was at the kitchen counter sorting through the day's mail while Lionel was at the table enjoying a cup of tea. Smyrna turned around and held up an envelope for her husband to see. "Here it is. It arrived on time."

"Aunt Sheila's letter?"

"Yup." Smyrna opened the envelope. "She'll be here in eight weeks." She handed the letter to Lionel. "May 5 to be exact. At least we have time to get ready."

Lionel looked up at Smyrna. "I wish we didn't have to go through this every year."

"I know dear. But it's the right thing to do."

He read the letter silently. "It's obvious she really appreciates our hospitality." Handing the letter back to Smyrna he continued, "and she adores Mary and Annie. They're the daughters she never had. But you know, when she's here, I get so exasperated. Gosh, that dog tracks dirt all over the place, and he sheds like crazy. And those animals get snot all over our windows! I can deal with the stuff she brings. It's the chaos and mess that bug me."

"I know," Smyrna said. "I hate seeing our lawn torn up by that pig and cow. It's hard on the girls, too. Everything about Aunt Sheila is such a huge embarrassment to them: the truck and trailer in the driveway, the animals, and everything else."

"I know. They keep their friends at bay when she's here," Lionel added.

"But she's family," Smyrna said with some finality.

Five weeks to the day after Aunt Sheila's letter had arrived the family was eating dinner when a loud knock at the door startled everyone.

"Who could that be?" Lionel wiped his mouth with a napkin, got up, and walked over to peer through the peep hole. "Who on earth?"

"Dear, who is it?" Smyrna asked.

"I don't know. I've never seen him before." Lionel opened the door enough to stick his head outside. "Yes, may I help you?"

"You Lyle?" the stranger asked.

"I'm Lionel. May I help you?"

The stranger took off his faded green driver's cap, removed his worn gloves, and held out his hand to shake Lionel's. Lionel stepped outside and shook the man's thick, weathered hand.

"John Shird. Next farm to Sheila."

"I'm pleased to meet you." Lionel noticed the stranger's pick-up truck parked on the street. In the passenger seat was a dog that looked a lot like Wisenheimer the Weimaraner.

"Brought the dog. Sheila wanted you to have 'im."

"She wanted me to have him?"

"Yup."

"She doesn't want him anymore?"

"Couldn't take 'im with her."

"She went somewhere?" The stranger's terse answers were confusing Lionel.

"Big farm," he said.

"She's moved?" Lionel asked.

The stranger looked at Lionel as if he was a fool. "Up thar," he said emphatically, pointing to the sky.

It suddenly dawned on Lionel what the man was saying. "Oh my God. Please come in, please. I'm so sorry." He opened the door and led Mr. Shird into the house.

Smyrna was up from the table and heading to the front door. She looked at her husband, "Dear, what's going on?"

"Honey, this is John Shird, Aunt Sheila's neighbor. I think she's passed away."

Smyrna looked anxiously at the farmer.

"Yup."

Lionel led Mr. Shird to the dining room table. "Please, sit down. Can we get you anything to eat?"

"I'd give you no objections mister," he said sitting down.

Smyrna returned to the table. Annie fixed a plate for food for the guest, and Mary got him a glass of water.

"What happened?" Smyrna asked.

"Long 'bout two weeks ago Sheila got worse." Mr. Shird drank some water. "Had ta take her to d' hospital. Doc told me wudn't much hope. Buried 'er a week later." Using a spoon, he took a mouth full of corn. "Sheila made me promise to get the dog to you. He's in the car. Herschel and Josephine gonna stay with me, less you need 'em."

"That's okay. They can stay with you," Smyrna said. "I had no idea she had been ill."

"She'd been fightin' a tumer 'bout two years."

"My word," Lionel said. "She never mentioned anything about this to us."

"That's her way. Didn't want nobody makin' no fuss."

Mr. Shird finished his dinner quietly while the family watched. He wiped his mouth, blew his nose with his napkin, and got up from the table. "I thank 'ee. I'll get the dog now and best be gone. Got a long drive ahead-a-me."

"You needn't go tonight," Lionel said. "Stay here with us and leave in the morning."

"Much obliged. But best be gone. Gotta feed them animals, sunrise."

Quietly, Mr. Shird walked out of the house, went to his pick-up, and returned with Wisenheimer the Weimaraner. Mary took the leash and led the dog to the bathtub. Annie followed close behind. Smyrna and Lionel escorted Mr. Shird to the door.

"Thank you so very much for coming. I'm sorry it had to be like this," Smyrna said.

"Sheila loved this here family. Talked 'bout you all the time." Mr. Shird headed out the door. Halfway to his truck he stopped and turned around. "Take good care of that dog. He's special."

On the evening of May 5, Smyrna, Lionel, Mary, and Annie were at the dining room table, and a freshly bathed Wisenheimer was on the floor, sound asleep. This particular night's meal was an unusually quiet affair, with few words spoken and almost no eye contact made. Finally, Smyrna broke the silence.

"Girls, I'm proud of the way you welcomed Aunt Sheila to this house. I know she was embarrassing to you, but you went along with her eccentricities anyway."

"I miss her, Mom," Annie said, crying.

"I can't believe she won't be here. I keep expecting to hear her truck pull into the driveway," Mary said. She, too, was in tears.

"I've got an idea," Lionel said with excitement in his voice. He got up and left the dining room. He returned several minutes later carrying the first of the five "Aunt Sheila's Visits" boxes. "Come on, everybody. Let's get ready for Aunt Sheila anyway!"

Mary, Annie, and Smyrna were shocked at first. The three looked at each other and then started smiling.

"Yes!" Smyrna said enthusiastically.

Annie and Mary returned to the basement with their father and helped him fetch the remaining four boxes. They carried them to the living room, and together the family sorted through the contents. Lionel pulled out a tie made from woven hay and held it up to his neck.

"I'm gonna wear this to work tomorrow."

The girls and their mother were laughing. Wisenheimer picked up the smell of his old home emanating from the boxes and wagged his tail, wildly.

Standing, Smyrna modeled a dress made from goat hair and decorated with dried flowers. She winked at her husband. "Care for a dance my love?"

"Where's that vest she made me?" Mary had her head buried in one of the boxes. "I want to wear it to school!"

"I thought you hated that thing," her sister said.

"Look, here's the baseball mitt she made for you, Annie." Lionel tossed the hand-made glove to his daughter.

By evening's end Lionel, Smyrna, Mary, Annie, and Weisenheimer had gone through the boxes and had prepared the house for the visit that wasn't to be. With an extra-large bowl of popcorn, they then sat in the living room and shared their memories of Aunt Sheila, filling the night with both tears and laughter.

Lionel let out a deep sigh. "Gosh, I'll miss that woman," he said.

Smyrna put her arm around her husband. "Me, too." She paused for a moment, jumped up, and then clapped her hands, "I've got a great idea! Let's do this every year!"

Lionel and the children looked at her with disbelief.

"You mean go through these boxes every year?" he asked.

"Yes, exactly," she said, excitedly.

Annie and Mary looked at each other. "Yes, yes," they screamed. "It'll be a riot!"

"I love it," Lionel said. "Let's do it!"

And so that night, in the home of Lionel, Smyrna, Mary, Annie, and Wisenheimer, a tradition was born. The evening of May 5 became a celebration that was to pass from one generation to the next. Every year this family gathered, with some even coming from across the country and still others from across the ocean. After a meal of kale, collard greens, chard, and scrapple and after sharing gifts made from things found around the house and out in the yard, they would honor the memory of this woman through embellished stories of her life and times. To this celebration they gave the name "The Night of Aunt Sheila's Visit," an occasion to celebrate life itself and bask in the love and history that bound them all together.

"I'm strangely warmed," Ken said.

"But what do y'all think of my message?" Billy asked.

"I feel the same as Ken. That was a strong message about the family, and feeling strangely warmed after hearing such a story is pure Wesleyan Ken, through and through," Jim added.

"Wesleyan? I'm sitting over the heater."

Sarah cut into the conversation. "Well Billy, you warmed my heart. But what's with the scrapple?"

"Nobody actually eats that stuff, do they?" Jim asked.

"What is scrapple, anyway?" Ed asked.

"It's a pork thing," Billy explained

"It's got corn meal in it, too," Ben added

"And a lot of other things too, I hear. Bob said. "Things I can't mention in front of the ladies."

"Ladies?" May said. "What century are you from?"

"Ed, let me tell you about scrapple. Scrapple is a lot like us. There's some stuff in it that ain't so bad and other stuff that's . . . well. . . you don't wanna know where it came from," Billy explained.

"The truth is, we are all people of scrapple," Bob pointed out. "We're all a mixture of good and bad stuff. It's theological"

"Speak for yourself!" Princeton said. "I, for one, would not eat it nor do I think it is theological."

"On that note, let's please move on." Dave wanted to get to the next tale. "I think the story was simply beautiful. I dare say, we are not far apart when it comes to family values."

"Thank you," Rev. Bending replied, taking a bow. "This is what family values are all about. The family should bring us together."

"Instead, they seem to divide us," Rev. Tucker added.

"Or worse," Sarah said. "Some of our fellow preachers use them to hack away at folks. It makes me sick."

"Scrapple's what makes me feel sick," Ron joked. "I know all about that stuff."

"Look, forget the scrapple. I'm sorry I brought it up," Billy said as he sat down next to his Baptist colleagues. "Next time I'll use hamburger paddies."

"Then you'd lose your theological grounding," Dave said. "You were truly quite profound."

"I wasn't trying to be profound," Billy said. "I was making a simple point."

"Amen!" Ben and Bob echoed. "That's the Baptist way!"

"We'd better keep going," Dave said. "We've heard from three, there're nine more to go and we've already passed Columbus!"

Ron Morgan was next to step forward with a story to share.

"My text is Luke 10:29," Ron said with Scripture in hand. "It's one we all know by heart: 'And who is my neighbor?'" He closed his Bible and continued, "My illustration of this text is a story I call 'The Church Mouse Academy.'"

"I hope it ain't bone-dry like a Princeton sermon!" Billy Barker said jokingly.

"Like your head, perhaps there will be a point to it," Princeton snapped back.

"Enough you two," Dave interrupted. "Ron, I for one want to hear you tale!"

And so, Ron began his story.

The Church Mouse Academy

But wanting to justify himself, he asked Jesus,
"And who is my neighbor?

(Luke 10:29 NRSV)

Caitlin O'Clannahy, a student of sacred music in her final year of seminary, was sound asleep. Well, not exactly sound asleep. Suffice it to say she was not awake. Caitlin's bed was one of four remaining original beds used at Blakely's own Good God Almighty Theological Seminary, an historic institution founded on August 28, 1856. With 160 years of service, the mattress had become so soft it resembled a hammock strung between two sagging loblolly pine trees. Thus, for Caitlin, deep sleep was problematic.

On this night, Caitlin was snapped to consciousness by some rustling noises. She got out of bed, found her flashlight, and searched the room for the source of this disturbance. In a corner, along the baseboard, she noticed several pieces of walnut.

"I don't remember eating any walnuts," she thought, getting on her hands and knees to examine the nuts.

Finding nothing else, she made a note to call administration about the noises and then got back into bed. Caitlin would soon discover that beneath the seminary's campus there existed not just a clumsy rodent but an entire theological institution for mice. The school, called Church Mouse Academy, was founded on August 29, 1856.

While it is not inconceivable that a larger creature could find the Church Mouse Academy, it certainly helps to be only four inches tall. You must first enter the right drainpipe underneath the Good God Almighty Theological Seminary's north lawn. Where it connects with the main south side drain spout, there's a small opening that leads through the broken side of an old half-buried dark grey cinder block. Once past the cinder block, you will see three small holes. You enter the one on the far-left side and make a sharp left turn after you pass under the root of the beautiful old oak tree. The tunnel then leads to an opening under the northwest basement window of the seminary's administration building. To get to the academy, you enter the opening, veer right, and follow the copper water pipe until it turns up into the floor above you. It is there on your left that you will see the academy's entrance. Above the door, in English, Greek, and Latin are the words (and academy motto), "Quiet as a Church Mouse."

The academy's headmaster, Dr. Cicero T. Pocket III, was very pleased with the senior class of students. Well, that is, with the exception of Horace. In more than one hundred and sixty years, no mouse had ever failed to graduate to a life of service as a church mouse. And this was a record of which the academy was very proud. Dr. Pocket feared that Horace would end this long-standing achievement. It's not that Horace did not try hard or that he was not smart enough to do the work. No, the young mouse's grades were better than average. Dr. Julius T. Field, the distinguished professor of Catmatics, gave Horace an A+ on his last term paper. The renowned scholar and historian, Dr. Agripina T. Harvest, ranked him among her top students. No, Horace faced an even greater challenge. In simple lay-mouse terms, he was a klutz and seemingly never would be "quiet as a church mouse."

One Friday afternoon, following a quiet and uplifting chapel service, Dr. Pocket decided to have a heart-to-heart chat with young Horace. He found the student's clumsiness deeply troubling. The Friday before, Horace had toppled the teacup used as a baptismal font. Earlier that same day he had dropped his lunch of acorns, walnut pieces, and cheese outside on the seminary lawn. Distracted and lost in thought, he then carelessly left them as he went on his way. To Dr. Pocket, the arrival of the bumble bee-colored exterminator's truck on Monday morning was a warning sign: The administrators of Good God Almighty Theological Seminary just might be suspicious of their presence. Horace, he feared, was like a clarion.

The two met in the headmaster's dusty, cluttered office, filled from floor to ceiling with old books, backdated journals, and yellowing articles clipped from long forgotten publications. A discarded mouse pad served as a rug and added a great deal of warmth to what would have otherwise been a very chilly room.

"Horace, Horace, Horace," the aging Headmaster said. "What am I to do with you?"

His heart sinking, Horace feared what was coming. "Father will be so disappointed in me," he thought.

"You're a smart mouse. You have a good heart. But I'm not so sure you belong here." Dr. Pocket continued, "The life of a church mouse is one that requires special gifts, the most important of which is a mastery of 'Quietude.' We must lead others to this way of life. God has not granted this gift to everyone. And I am certain you understand, a church mouse serves where humans gather." His cheek pouches drooping, Horace looked down at the floor. "Do you truly want to stay here?"

"Yes sir, I do," Horace replied.

Dr. Pocket let out a long sigh. "Let me give it some thought, my son."

Horace lived in Dorm B. More specifically, he lived in a small but cozy space beneath the floor of Room B-222, now occupied by Caitlin O'Clannahy. It was Caitlin's complaint that led to the subsequent arrival of the technicians from Bug-Off Exterminators last Monday morning. Being committed users of snap traps with cheese bait, Bug-Off proved to be ineffectual since nearly all church mice now know to avoid these contraptions. In any event, the students and faculty at the Church Mouse Academy knew they needed to make an extra effort to put their Quietude into practice.

That Friday afternoon Horace made the round-about journey back to his cozy space. His meeting with Dr. Cicero T. Pocket III, however, left him even more distracted than usual. Instead of making two rights and a left after passing through the second-floor hole in the elevator shaft, Horace made one right and two left turns, thus dropping himself smack in the middle of Caitlin's dorm room floor, where at that very moment, as fate would have it, she was coming through the door.

"Ahyeeeee!" she screamed, tossing up into the air a ten-volume Theological Dictionary.

Like Horace, Caitlin was having a bad day. As a matter of fact, this particular Friday had topped off a particularly bad week as well as a particularly bad month. Also, like Horace, Caitlin had had a heart-to-heart chat with someone about her seminary career. In her case it was with one of her teachers, the Most Exceedingly and Highly Right Rev. Dr. Tedius P.

Hardscrabble, the esteemed and pre-eminent professor of Circumlocutious Theology.

Caitlin O'Clannahy was from an Atlanta subdivision called Dairy Air, one of those far-flung neighborhoods attached to the city by a forever-clogged arterial highway. She came to Good God Almighty Theological Seminary following a twelve-year career in the chronically under-funded Cherokee County public school system, where she taught dance and music to boys and girls. Caitlin, who was dearly loved by all her students as well as their parents, didn't actually work in one school. Instead, she divided her time among the forty-odd elementary schools scattered about the county. Caitlin loved music of all kinds, from the passion-filled symphonies of Bach to the car-rattling vibrations of urban hip-hop. Yet, her real dream was to direct a cathedral choir or to lead a troupe of liturgical dancers. This is why she enrolled in the Sacred Music Program at Good God Almighty Theological Seminary. She had not, however, envisioned Dr. Hardscrabble and his required two-part, year-long course, "Inappreciable, Inconceptible, and Inexplicable Immateriality."

It was Caitlin's scream that woke Horace from his daydream, and it was the ten-volume theological dictionary she was juggling that prevented his escape. Volume ten landed on his tail, pinning it to the floor, while volumes one through nine surrounded him like a fortress wall. With every bit of the agility of young a young Bolshoi ballerina, Caitlin leapt into the air and landed fully upright on her seminary bed. But the old and dry nineteenth century wooden slats were equally agile. They gave way and spilled her onto the floor. And this was where they met, human and mouse, face-to-face.

It's hard to judge exactly how long Caitlin and Horace stared at each other. It may have been only a minute, but it seemed more like an hour. For that instant it was as if time stopped, as if Good God Almighty Theological Seminary and Church Mouse Academy faded into a distant mist and all ages, past and present, merged into one solitary moment. And deep in their eyes, Caitlin and Horace sensed a need for each other, that somehow this very event had been foreordained, that from this day forward their lives would be forever joined.

Horace broke the silence. "My tail kind of hurts. Could you move this book, please?" Caitlin lifted the plump volume and freed the little mouse.

"It's not broken or anything, is it?" she asked.

Horace felt his tail and wiggled it bit. "It seems okay. What about your bed?"

"I guess I'll have to call the maintenance people." Caitlin looked over her shoulder at the torn mattress and tangled mass of splintered wood and then at the rather large bruise forming on her right knee.

"Ooh, that looks awful," Horace said, looking at her knee.

Turning back to Horace, Caitlin introduced herself, "By the way, I'm Caitlin O'Clannahy."

Horace got up and with his front paws carefully brushed off his shoulders and white tummy. "I'm Horace." He looked at the ten-volume theological dictionary. "That can be a tough read," he said.

"Tell me about it," replied Caitlin. "If Dr. Hardscrabble doesn't pass me this semester, I'll never get out of here. You know, I don't recall those recruitment people ever mentioning this Immaterial Theology thing. I hate it!"

Glancing about the room, Horace saw a collection of DVDs, a guitar, a flute, a recorder, and quite a few books on music-related themes. On her walls were an assortment of posters: pictures of famous composers, souvenirs from concerts and festivals, and announcements of recitals. "Actually," Horace replied. "I like theology. As a matter of fact, it's one of my favorite subjects."

"But it's so confusing," Caitlin countered. "I can't even figure out where to begin. It's like trying to catalog a huge pile of sand!"

"Okay, I'll grant you it can be a bit tedious. But on the other paw, theology is all about relationships—with God and God's creation. I think it's most intriguing."

By now the sun was setting, and both Caitlin and Horace were feeling the pangs of hunger. "I'll make dinner," Caitlin offered with her usual grace and generous spirit. She got up from the floor and headed to her dresser. In addition to having an original bed, Caitlin's room included the other original pieces of furniture supplied to the students of Good God Almighty Theological Seminary way back in 1856—a tall dresser, a small desk, and one wooden chair. The top drawer of her dresser served as the pantry. The small refrigerator next to the dresser was a gift from her brother, and the microwave on top came from her aunt. She had bought the toaster oven on top of the microwave for $3.50 at a yard sale. The hot plate situated atop the toaster oven was on loan from her older sister, and the mug sitting on it was a reward from her bank for opening a checking account.

"Let me see what we've got here." Caitlin opened the top drawer and found an apple, two cans of corn, one of green beans, and a box of saltine crackers. "Hmmm," she sighed. She opened the refrigerator and found cheddar cheese, some milk, and a jar of Spanish olives. "I hope you don't mind eclectic."

"I love corn. Crackers and cheese are great. I'll take milk too," Horace said, happy at the thought of eating. Caitlin heated some corn and with a hodgepodge of other foodstuffs, set up a picnic meal on her dorm room floor. She poured some milk into a thimble and handed it to Horace, who promptly dropped it, spilling the contents into the bowl of corn. While trying to pick up the thimble, he lost his footing and landed squarely on the plate of cheese. Horace got up and accidently backed into the olives.

"Horace, why don't you let me help you."

"I'm so sorry. What a klutz I am. I'll never make it through the academy," Horace muttered.

"Academy? What are you talking about?" asked Caitlin.

"Oops."

In the back of her mind Caitlin had been a bit puzzled over Horace's interest in esoteric theology. After all, that's not something one normally associates with a mouse. His last comment piqued her interest. "Tell me, what's this about an academy?"

"I'm not supposed to tell you anything about it," replied Horace. "Church Mouse Academy is a secret."

"Are you telling me that there's a school for mice here, at Good God Almighty Theological Seminary?"

Horace was getting frazzled. "There's nothing beneath the Administration Building that you should know about."

"How many mice are there? And where do they live?" Caitlin's curiosity was growing very quickly.

"Oh dear!" Beneath the fur, Horace's cheek pouches were getting quite red. "I can't tell you. It's not like we make a lot of noise here."

Caitlin pressed him for more information. "Are you telling me you live here, in this residence hall?"

Now Horace was hyperventilating. "Oh, dear me! It's a secret."

"My little mouse, you've already spilled the beans." Sensing Horace's extreme discomfort, Caitlin stopped pushing him. "Look, I promise you, I won't say anything to anyone, ever." Believing Caitlin, Horace began to relax.

After they finished their picnic, Caitlin cleaned up, and they continued to talk well into the wee hours of the morning. Horace told her all about Dr.

Pocket and the headmaster's concern over his clumsiness. Likewise, Caitlin spoke of her trepidation about Dr. Hardscrabble and his most grueling and mind-boggling course. By the time the sun's first rays appeared, a mutual admiration and love that was to last a lifetime had been born. On a more practical note, Caitlin and Horace committed themselves to helping each other over their seemingly insurmountable hurdles.

The following Saturday morning Horace met Caitlin in her dorm room. "Horace, have you ever heard of Gene Kelly? My God, could he ever dance! I don't think any dancer has matched his athletic ability."

"I can't say that I have," Horace replied.

Caitlin continued, "I think men are afraid of dancing. I don't know why. Some denominations even demonize it. Anyway, I think learning to dance could help you get control of your clumsiness." Caitlin rummaged through her collection of DVDs and found a copy of *Singin' in the Rain*. "Watch this," she said as she inserted the disc and fast-forwarded to her favorite scene. Horace was entranced. He had never seen anything like it. "You see the way he moves his body with the music? It becomes part of him. Every motion flows with the rhythm of the song." She stopped the DVD and then put on a Glenn Miller CD. Rolling up the carpet remnant, she directed Horace, "Here, stand up. Close your eyes and just listen to the music. Tap you paw to the beat. . . one-two-three-four. . . one-two-three-four. . . one-two-three-four."

Horace got up and, putting his left back paw forward, tried tapping in time with the beat. By four o'clock he was doing the jitterbug.

The next Wednesday found Horace back in Caitlin's room. This time he was the tutor. "Go over to your window Caitlin and look outside. Tell me what you see."

Caitlin walked over to the old double-hung window and hoisted the lower sash. Resting her arms on the sill, she replied, "I see gothic buildings, cars passing by the brick sidewalks. Ummm. I see people hurrying around in different directions. There are two women playing tennis and, oh yes, that beautiful old oak tree."

"Now get your Bible and let's start at the beginning. Tell me what you see."

Caitlin took her Bible and opened it to the book of Genesis. "I see stories. I see God getting angry. I see genealogies. . . I see. . . What else is there to see?" she asked.

"Pick any chapter, Caitlin, and read aloud."

She turned to chapter 26 and read, "Now there was famine in the land. . ." She continued reading all the way to the final verse of the chapter. She looked at Horace blankly. "I don't get what it has to do with me."

"Don't you see," Horace remarked. "It's so visual. As you read, imagine what the people were wearing and what they were doing. Imagine what the buildings looked like. Then think of what it was like if you were hungry or if you were in trouble. Let the text breathe and the people in it come alive. Don't analyze it; visualize it! This is where it all begins!"

Week after week their tutoring sessions continued, and their friendship deepened. With a little time and a whole lot of help from Horace, Caitlin's fear of Dr. Hardscrabble slowly evaporated. Her self-assurance improved as she discovered a growing appreciation for theology, even the immaterial kind. With Caitlin's dance lessons, Horace's confidence grew, and his clumsiness became less apparent. For Horace, liturgy was becoming something of wondrous beauty and less a great obstacle to his ordination as a church mouse.

At last, the month of May arrived, and with it final examinations and, hopefully, graduation. Caitlin's last and most difficult test fell on a Tuesday. At 9:00 in the morning, she sat at her classroom desk and opened the test-book. There was only one very, very short question that drew upon everything that had ever been discussed and/or read in "Inappreciable Inconceptible, and Inexplicable Immateriality." It drew upon every lecture, every article, and every book ever written by the Most Exceedingly and Highly Right Rev. Dr. Tedius P. Hardscrabble. She knew that no word, no sentence, no paragraph that had ever emanated from the head of this esteemed and pre-eminent scholar could be overlooked. Caitlin wiped the nervous sweat from her forehead, said a short prayer, and silently looked at the one-word exam question: "Why"

At 4:32 in the afternoon, Caitlin put down her pen and rubbed her aching wrist. She was finished. With great pride, she got up, walked down the aisle, and placed her test-book squarely on the table, next to the snoring Dr. Hardscrabble. For seven and one-half hours, Caitlin had poured herself into the examination. Now that it was over, she felt as if someone had vacuumed out every conscious thought from her head. Yet Caitlin knew she had passed. All she wanted to do now was to find Horace and kiss his furry cheek. He had saved her sacred music career.

Horace was in Caitlin's dorm room preparing for the Liturgical Quietude final scheduled for Wednesday morning. Dr. Pocket and the entire faculty, as well as the whole student body of the Church Mouse Academy, were anxiously awaiting the young mouse's performance the next day. They were wondering, would he topple the baptismal teacup again? Would he drop the communion thimble? Would he fumble the toothpick crosier? Would he be the cause of the academy's discovery? Like a rodent Gene Kelly, Horace moved back and forth, from side to side, and round the perimeter of Caitlin's room. The tango was his favorite. But then the sound of a key in the lock sent him scurrying for cover.

Entering her room, Caitlin whispered as loudly as she could, "Horace, are you here?" The little mouse peered from around the footboard of Caitlin's rebuilt bed. "I did it! I did it! I did it! I passed!" Caitlin said.

Horace smiled. "Your ability is light years ahead of your self-confidence. But I always knew you could do it."

"Have you been practicing for your exam?" Caitlin asked.

Horace looked down at his feet. Wiggling his toes he replied, "You were right, liturgy is a sort of dance, and that tango is a lot like a high church procession! I just hope the rest of me cooperates."

Wednesday morning found Horace and several of his classmates in the narthex of the Church Mouse Academy chapel waiting for the Liturgical Quietude examination. He was wearing a freshly starched vestment Caitlin had made for him from one of the handkerchiefs she had inherited from her grandmother. This was a special occasion, and she wanted Horace to look the part. When the music began, Horace held his head up high. He closed his eyes and imagined he was in a Buenos Aires nightclub. He took a deep breath, grabbed the toothpick crosier, and began his march down the aisle. Every eye was on Horace. From the moment he entered the chapel until the moment he reached the altar, no mouse took a breath, uttered the slightest whisper, or twitched even the smallest whisker. Horace set the crosier in its stand and reached for the communion thimble. With both front paws he lifted it into the air, piercing a small cloud of incense. Horace looked at a cross hanging near the altar and smiled. He knew he had reached Quietude. Horace turned to face the congregation, again lifted the communion thimble into the air, and said the famous prayer of that great pocket-mouse who lived in the walls of New York's Union Theological Seminary: "Holy God, creator of all there is, make us invisible to those who would harm us, make us visible to those who would need us, and grant us the wisdom to distinguish the one from the other."

When the Liturgical Quietude examination was over, Horace marched back down the aisle. His little heart was soaring. "I did it!" he said to himself.

Dr. Cicero T. Pocket III could not believe his eyes. In all his years as headmaster no student of the Church Mouse Academy had ever exhibited such grace and agility with Liturgical Quietude. Dr. Pocket followed Horace into the narthex. "Horace, Horace, Horace. That was simply beautiful, just beautiful, wonderfully beautiful. You have the gift."

Horace's eyes welled with tears. "Thank you, sir," he replied.

One-week later Horace received his diploma. As always, commencement ceremonies were held deep beneath Good God Almighty Theological Seminary's dining hall in the Church Mouse Academy's Secret Assembly Place. Horace's mom and dad as well as his 37 siblings were on hand to witness this proud moment. Dr. Cicero T. Pocket II, father of the current headmaster, gave a challenging though still very inspiring keynote address. After nearly two hours of wonderful music and beautiful liturgy, the graduating class of Church Mouse Academy knelt at the altar to be officially ordained. Dr. Cicero T. Pocket III, gently rested his paws between the ears of each mouse while Dr. Cicero T. Pocket II whispered the traditional ordination prayer: "Wherever you go, bring peace, teach safety, and share our great tradition."

Horace was now a Church Mouse. With great pomp and circumstance, he and his classmates marched down the aisle in one long single-file precession. Before leaving the Secret Assembly Place, Horace spotted his mom and dad. They smiled at him. And with that one gesture came a revelation. It wasn't what he had or would accomplish that made them happy. No, it was the joy they saw in him. For his mom and Dad, that was enough to engender their pride.

Caitlin received her diploma the following day. Her aunt, brother, and older sister packed up the silver Volvo wagon and reluctantly made the trip from Dairy Air to attend Good God Almighty Theological Seminary's graduation ceremony. Dr. Hardscrabble had been scheduled to deliver the commencement address. However, facing the very real threat of a student boycott, Dean Howie B. Stockstill DD, PhD quietly slipped in a replacement speaker: the Utmost Rev. Dr. Olduvai Bone, Professor of Church Administration. His address, "Managing Operational Liabilities in the Mid-Cap Suburban Congregation," had Caitlin's family (and everyone else) fidgeting long before his closing remarks.

After the orderly and sedate graduation service, Caitlin caught up with her aunt, brother, and older sister in the parking lot just as they were about to climb into the Volvo. They were in a hurry and wanted to get back to Dairy Air for their favorite TV programs. Caitlin managed to give each one a kiss before they closed the doors.

As her aunt was revving up the engine, Caitlin's sister rolled the window down and motioned for her to come near. "How much longer will you need my hot plate?" she wanted to know. "I like it a lot."

Forcing a smile, Caitlin said, "Not long."

Her aunt stomped on the gas pedal and the vehicle sped off, leaving Caitlin alone in the parking lot. In the distance, near the beautiful old oak tree, she could see her classmates, their families, guests, and the seminary faculty beginning the traditional covered dish farewell brunch. Caitlin then thought about Horace. "I wonder how he's doing."

The day before Horace had mentioned that immediately after ordination all Church Mice headed off for a month of solitude and quiet reflection to a place even more secret than the Church Mouse Academy. Caitlin felt sad that she had not had the chance to say good-bye.

"I could use some comfort food," she thought. Skipping the covered dish celebration-brunch, Caitlin headed off campus to the old railroad-car-shaped Tastee Diner. There she ordered the three-vegetable carry-out dinner consisting of mashed potatoes with gravy, macaroni and cheese, black-eyed peas, and a complimentary corn muffin. "After I eat, I'll turn on some nice music, take a hot bath, and read a good book—that's what I need." She took the long way around the seminary, stopping by Fred's Used Books for a novel, and Anne's Bath Shop for lemon grass bath gel. She just needed a little time alone. Caitlin got to her room, put the key into the lock, and opened the door.

"Caitlin!" shouted Horace.

"Ahyeeeee!" she screamed tossing up into the air her three vegetable carry-out dinner, novel, and lemon grass bath gel.

Caitlin had not expected to see Horace. Horace had not expected to be buried in a mound of mashed potatoes, macaroni and cheese, black eyed peas, corn muffin, a book, and the contents of a bottle of bath gel.

"Horace, I'm so sorry." Caitlin picked him up and did her best to clean him.

"You don't do well with surprises, do you?" he said. As it turns out, Horace had several hours before it was time to leave, and he had come to say good-bye.

"Horace, I owe so much to you. I don't know what I would have done without you."

The mouse smiled. "And I, you. I must admit at first it was really tough. All my life I've been taught to distrust humans. You have proven to be an exception. I can trust you."

Caitlin sat down on the floor. "I was scared, too! I'd never met a mouse before. I had no idea what you all were like."

"How could you be afraid of me?" asked Horace. "We're the ones who have to hide."

The two talked for another hour, and then it was time for Horace to go. Caitlin wept. Horace wept too.

"Oh, my wonderful little mouse, I'll miss you terribly. "She said. "We have to stay connected."

"Somehow Caitlin, I think we always will," he replied, wiping his soggy eyes. "We always will." The good-byes continued for several minutes. Then Horace left the dorm room, leaving Caitlin alone.

Caitlin cleaned up the last vestige of her comfort food and looked out the window. Down below, the covered dish farewell brunch was in full swing. She could see Dr. Hardscrabble and Dean Stockstill; judging from their body language and the wild motions they were making with their hands, the two were arguing about something. She sighed, put on a shawl, left her room, and headed down to the gathering.

"I may as well get something to eat," she said to herself. Along the way Caitlin started humming "Singin' in the Rain." She smiled as she thought of Horace dancing round about her room. "God bless you, my friend, God bless you."

On the other side of campus in his dusty cluttered office beneath the seminary administration building, Dr. Cicero T. Pocket III was finishing the official Church Mouse ordination papers for this year's graduating class. He, too, was thinking of Horace.

"How did he do it?" he wondered aloud as he signed the last paper. He put away the special pen and got up from his desk. "I am most curious. I've never seen such rhythmical movements. I'll ask him when he gets back. Yes, yes, that is what I will do, I will inquire of him. Most curious, indeed," he muttered.

Dr. Pocket put on his tattered coat, turned off the light, and headed to the exit tunnel. "I'll bet that Horace has an exceptional story to share with me. Yes, I'll bet it's most exceptional."

After finishing his tale, Rev. Morgan returned to his seat.

"An exceptional tale," Princeton said, no pun intended. "But let us not lose sight of sound theological training. My knowledge is my ministry, and it is that that makes me and every one of us important to our congregations."

"Or impotent," Sue whispered to Ron.

"I heard that," snapped Princeton.

Ron jumped back into the conversation. "Look, before you go off the deep end, my point was that Caitlin and Horace helped each other cross a lot of deep barriers—of fear, of ignorance, and of. . ."

"And self-importance!" Sue cut in.

"Don't forget the barriers to learning that Caitlin had to cross," Princeton suggested, ignoring Sue. "We who speak on behalf of the Holy must know more than those who do not."

"I, for one, want to keep the ball rolling! I've had enough quibbling," Rev. Tucker said, putting the brakes on the interchange. "Who's next?"

"I am next," Rev. Leslie said. He went to take Ron's place up front and there read from John's gospel: "and you will know the truth, and the truth will make you free." Ken closed his Bible and put it on a bench. "My tale is different from the one I shared last year," he said. "This time it's meant to be funny. I call it, "The Offbase Incident," and it takes place near our own town of Blakely!"

The Offbase Incident

If you continue in my word, you are truly my disciples; and you will
know the truth, and the truth will make you free.

(JOHN 8:31–32 NRSV)

"AHHHHH! OH, MY GOD, ahhhhhh!"

Button Gwinnett Benson, Early County's sole taxicab driver, was hol-
lering louder than a cornered turkey on Thanksgiving eve. He had expected
to see a baloney sandwich and apple crisp in his padded lunch box. Instead,
he was staring into the vacant eye sockets of a human skull. He tossed the
lunch box back into his open trunk and screamed louder.

"Oh, my gosh, ahhhhh!"

Button was in the gravel parking lot of Jack's Porkeria, a diner serving
seventeen varieties of barbeque pork sandwiches. He had stopped to get a
side order of French fries and a soft drink to go with his lunch.

"What do I do now?" he whimpered. Button looked over his shoulder
and yelled, "Call the cops! Quick! Somebody's head's in my lunch box!"

Button had no idea that the original user of the skull had died some
125,000 years before in the present-day Mudgeon valley in southwestern
Germany. The skull, called Cro-Mudgeon Man, had been discovered by Dr.
Homer Habilis six months before and was supposed to be with the anthropologist and on its way to Baden-Baden for permanent display in the city's
new municipal museum. Dr. Habilis, heading to the World Anthropological

Society's yearly conference in Stuttgart, planned to pass through the city along the way so he could present the skull at a special dedication ceremony. Homer did not know he was traveling with Button's lunch and not the Cro-Mudgeon Man skull. Needless to say, quite a surprise awaited Dr. Habilis, Baden-Baden mayor Gerhard Hanswurst, Deutsche Welt TV personality Heidi Trottelhaus, and the entire audience that would assemble at Baden Baden Hall for the festivities.

The Cro-Mudgeon Man already had traveled more miles in the past six months than in the entire lifetime of its original owner—once across the Atlantic Ocean and seven hours in the trunk of an Early County taxicab. Button was the driver who had taken Dr. Habilis to the county airport at 5:00 a.m. for the first leg of a long journey to Stuttgart. Another significant fact is that both Button and Homer had purchased identical padded containers at Habersham's Department Store on the very same day. The anthropologist appreciated the thick top, bottom, and sides, which could function as safety cushions against possible damage to the contents while in transit. The taxi driver focused more on the container's insulating capabilities for keeping food warm or cold. In any event, rushing to catch his flight, Homer had grabbed the wrong container from Button's trunk.

Augustus C. Bacon, (or Stus as he was known in the community), the town of Offbase, Georgia's police officer, was enjoying a double deluxe barbeque sandwich at Jack's Porkeria when he heard Button screaming outside. He grabbed his Stetson hat, unsnapped the safety that held his revolver in its holster, and ran out the door, along with everyone else in the restaurant.

"I'm in control here!" he yelled as he tried to rush past two insurance agents, the Men's Lunchtime Prayer Club from Elbert Methodist Church, the Hueless Motors sales team, and fourteen clerks from city hall, all of whom, like Stus, had been dining at Jack's Porkeria and wanted to see what the ruckus was all about.

Button immediately raised both hands in the air; Stus was pointing his loaded revolver at the terrified cab driver. Behind the police officer, Button could see the lunchtime crowd, numbering some thirty-five persons, quickly forming a horseshoe-shaped row between Stus and the restaurant.

"I d-d-d-didn't d-d-do it, Sssssstus." This was Button Gwinnett Benson's first experience peering into the open end of a .36 caliber revolver and, needless to say, he was shaken. "II f-f-f-found th-th-th-the skullll in m-m-m-my trunk"

Stus put his gun back in the holster. "Oh Button, put your hands down. I ain't gonna shoot you." The officer walked to the open trunk to look inside. "I just had to secure the crime scene." He turned around and, in an irritated voice, yelled at the crowd: "Now all of you, move back! This here's a police operation. There ain't nothin' here that concerns any-a-you folks."

Lunchtime Prayer Club member Harold Lumpkin yelled back, "Hey Stus! What's Button got in his trunk?"

"Aw, Harold, go on back to lunch," Stus replied, feeling exasperated.

"He's got somebody's head!" Bess Elbert, one of the Porkeria servers, shouted.

"Don't ya need to deputize some of us?" Zebulon Pickens, another Prayer Club member, added. "If this here is a murder ya might could use some help."

"Like I said before," Stus responded, trying hard to be patient. "This is an official police operation. Go on back to lunch, all-a-you." Stus then looked at the open lunch box. "That's a skull, all right." He looked at Button. "What's it doin' in your trunk?" he asked.

"I got no idea," the cab driver replied. "I was gonna get my sandwich and dessert, and there it was."

Stus continued his line of questioning, "You know who it is. . .I mean, was?" Stus pulled a note pad from its belt-pouch and sharpened a pencil with his teeth.

"Can't say I recognize him," Button replied. "Could be anybody."

Taking notes, the officer returned his gaze to Cro-Mudgeon Man. "You know where the rest of him is?" he asked the cab driver.

Back in the crowd, Zebulon was still yelling. "Ain't you gonna 'rest Button?"

"Yeah," Bess shouted. "You should arrest 'im."

A dozen or so from the crowd voiced their agreement. "Arrest him, arrest him, arrest him," they shouted in unison

Frustrated, Stus turned around once more and glared at the crowd. "Now look here. Let's get one thing straight. Ain't nobody gonna get arrested til I get to the bottom of this," the officer said forcefully.

Zebulon yelled again, "My cousin's the chief of police in Valdosta. He woulda 'rested him by now!"

The crowd was making Button even more anxious. "All I did was find 'im in my trunk, Stus," he said, almost crying.

"They got you, Button. Caught you like a guinea hen!" Henry Hueless shouted.

The crowd joined in again, "Arrest him, arrest him, arrest him!"

"Don't lock me up, Stus. Please!" the cab driver pleaded.

"Button, like I said, I ain't gonna arrest you," Stus replied, trying to calm him. "But you'd best stay in town 'til this is over."

"He's gonna run," Harold Lumpkin predicted. "You mark my words."

Officer Bacon took the skull and container from Button's trunk and headed to his patrol car. Zebulon, Harold, Bess, Henry, and the lunchtimers from Jack's Porkeria followed at a safe distance.

"You got the head of Sam Butts in that box," Harold yelled. "That's what I think."

Bess followed, "You think Button beaned Butts?"

"Button beaned Butts, Button beaned Butts," the crowd chanted.

Now in his car, Stus rolled the window down and addressed the crowd: "First, nobody knows if this is Sam's head. Second, you don't know if Button killed 'im. Third, go back inside and finish your lunch."

The officer started the car, flipped on the siren and the whirling blue lights and, in a cloud of dust and bits of flinging gravel, sped out of the driveway.

"Wee-oh, wee-oh, wee-oh." With sirens screaming and the wind rushing through the open windows, an exhilarated officer Bacon zoomed down Highway 15. Several cows looked up briefly and then continued munching their grass.

"Finally, a homicide," he said to himself. "Just hope I ain't got no statute limitations."

Officer Bacon turned into the police headquarters parking lot and skidded to a stop. The wooden screen door slapping behind him, he entered the white clapboard building that has served as police H.Q. for five generations. He said hello to Officer Nancy Jenkins, the other half of the force, and headed into his office. Stus placed the padded container on his desk and carefully lifted the skull out, setting it on the old black blotter. He switched on his desk lamp and aimed it directly at Cro-Mudgeon Man.

"Nancy, come in here! Look at this!"

Stus settled back into his old wooden, wheeled chair—used by his father and grandfather—and examined the ancient head.

"You been without a face quite a while," he said to the Cro-Mudgeon man. "I'll bet you died at least five years ago."

Nancy walked into the office as Stus picked at the back of his neck. "Sam Butts's been missing 'bout five years, ain't that right?" he asked her. "A week shy a' five years," officer Jenkins replied. "You think that's him?" "Could be."

Stus carefully examined the padded container. While holding a magnifying glass to his left eye, he noticed the corner of a manila card stuck under the container's plastic frame, between the vinyl side and first layer of foam. He pulled at it until it came loose. It was a business card that read, *Homer Habilis PhD, Professor of Paleoanthropology, Early College.* Stus pushed back from his desk and said, "Now this is gettin' interesting."

Homer Habilis had earned his doctoral degree in paleoanthropology at Georgia State University five years ago, and Early College was his first teaching appointment. The college itself sits square in the middle of Offbase, Georgia, a town so named because it lies at the edge of the U.S. Army's Fort Blakely, home of that elite, ultra-secret fighting force, the Green Fedoras.

Officer Bacon had a hunch Homer's arrival bore some relation to Sam's disappearance. He was right on that point, partially. Sam Butts had left his Chevette in his brother Amos's driveway and for six months never bothered to move it. Then when his brother was nowhere to be found, Amos sold it to the newly arrived and unwitting Homer.

"I may as well get some cash for that car," Amos figured. "Sam obviously doesn't want it no more." Amos also figured nobody would notice if he forged Sam's signature on the county vehicle registration document. On that point, he was wrong. Officer Bacon, for one, did notice.

Homer made matters worse for himself by forgetting to transfer the car's registration and by choosing to be out of the country when Stus found his business card buried in a case that contained a skull. Nor was Homer helped when Amos and his wife, fleeing bill collectors, joined a missionary group headed for Papua, New Guinea just when the anthropologist needed a corroborating witness.

Searching Homer's house, Stus and Nancy found the Chevette keys, the car registration papers with Sam's forged signature, a toiletry kit in the bathroom, and on the kitchen counter, a plastic baggie containing what appeared to be a controlled substance of a recreational nature. To the forensic eye of Stus, the toiletry kit and baggie proved that Homer was a drug dealer who had fled in a hurry. After all, if the departure had occurred with any forethought, obviously he would have taken his toothbrush, razor, and deodorant. And to Stus, the forged Chevette registration papers provided a motive—Sam's car had been stolen, likely because of unpaid drug debts. Taken together, these clues pointed to one thing and only one thing: Illegal narcotics and gangland warfare had come to Offbase, Georgia.

Meanwhile, over in Germany, Homer was on his way to Baden-Baden for the Cro-Mudgeon Man presentation ceremony, a very important event for everyone involved. To Homer Habilis, it was a moment in the limelight with his new discovery; to Gerhard Hanswurst, an opportunity to impress the electorate; to Heidi Trottelhaus, a chance to wow the evening news producers in Stuttgart; and to the three hundred townsfolk assembled in Baden-Baden's Baden-Baden Hall, a chance to get some free strudel.

The audience sat in ten evenly spaced rows, each consisting of thirty very clean metal folding chairs. A wooden stage with a lectern and display table had been constructed the day before. Upon this stage sat Homer, Gerhard, and Heidi. In Homer's lap sat Button's lunch; in Gerhard's, a pet cat named Attila; and in Heidi's, questions for an interview with Homer.

Not long after the three took their seats, the mayor's cat caught a whiff of the now-aging baloney. Attila leapt from Gerhard onto Homer's lap and like a starved lion furiously tried to open the padded container. Homer pushed her onto the floor several times, but the tenacious cat kept jumping back. She then managed to hook one of her claws in the zipper and as luck would have it, was unable to pull herself free. Startled, she howled and tried to back away from Homer, who at the same time was doing his best to hold onto the padded container. Attila dug her hind claws into Dr. Habilis's thigh and with all her strength, made one final thrust backwards. The cat pulled the container from Homer's protective grasp, sailed into the crowd and landed on the head of hairdresser Helga Kopf. Helga jumped to her feet, spilling the cat and padded container onto the ground. With her claw still stuck in the zipper, Attila spun in wildly erratic circles, trying to work herself free. Knowing Attila's reputation, the frightened audience backed away, some falling over the chairs as they fled to safety. With her claw still stuck in the zipper, the spinning Attila flew out of an open window and landed in the middle of a twelfth century courtyard.

With an angry Atilla still moving in circles, the padded container finally separated from her claw, flew over a ten-foot medieval town wall, rolled down a long hill, and then dropped off a small cliff into the River Oos. Gerhard and Homer left the stage and ran to the window where they watched the padded container on its journey into the Oos and on its way to the great Rhine River, just a few kilometers away. Both Gerhard and Homer had a bad feeling that their reputations and career prospects were going downstream with the container.

Meanwhile the disappointed attendees exited Baden-Baden Hall while Heidi did her best to salvage the day. She had twenty minutes remaining in her live broadcast and did what any fledgling journalist watching a career slip into oblivion would do: She talked. Heidi talked about Cro-Mudgeon Man, the Oos and other lesser-known tributaries of the Rhine, why Baden-Baden is Baden-Baden and not simply Baden, the weather—anything to fill in what felt hours and hours separating her from the top of the hour.

Following the World Anthropological Society meeting in Stuttgart, Homer flew back to Georgia. As his plane taxied to Gate 1½ at the Early County airport, he noticed a dozen or so police cars on the tarmac with their lights flashing.

"Goodness. Something must be up," he said to a passenger seated next to him.

Already feeling depressed about losing the only known Cro Mudgeon Man skull, Homer stepped off the plane and walked to the airport gate. He was shocked at the number of state and county police officers. He also saw Officer Augustus C. Bacon from Offbase. Homer turned to a stranger walking next to him and said, "There must have been some criminal on our plane." He looked all around to see who it might be.

Stus and Nancy marched up to Homer. In a stern voice Stus ordered the anthropologist to stop.

"Homer Habilis, I'm arresting you for the murder of Sam Butts."

Nancy read Homer his Miranda rights.

Depressed and exhausted from the long flight, his knees shaking, and every other part of him in a state of complete shock, Dr. Habilis could only say, "Huh?"

The Offbase, Georgia grapevine spread like mildew in a damp bathroom. By dinner time nearly everyone in the city had heard that the anthropologist was charged with murder. A crowd of fifty citizens had gathered outside the clapboard police H.Q. where Homer took up temporary residence in one of the small cinderblock cells. Harold Lumpkin, Zebulon Pickens, and several other people tried to peek through the windows to catch a glimpse of the man whom everyone thought had beaned Butts.

"Y'all gonna go for the death penalty?" Harold yelled.

"My cousin in Valdosta woulda had 'im fried!" Zebulon added.

Someone else in the crowd got everyone chanting, "Death, death, death to the killer."

Inside the jail Homer was meeting with his court-appointed attorney, Janice Hillmen. "I didn't kill anyone," he told her again and again. "I'm so relieved that I didn't lose the skull, but you have to understand it's ancient. It's not Butts."

"I believe you, Homer," she replied. The noise of the crowd outside was loud enough to make holding a conversation difficult. But Janice continued anyway, "Each piece of evidence they have won't hold water by itself. But the prosecutor's going to use them together to paint a picture that ties you to Sam Butts."

Homer protested. "Any anthropologist will confirm that it's a prehistoric fossil and could not be Sam Butts!"

"I know that, Homer," Janice replied. "And we will be using our own expert witnesses. But remember, there'll be folks in the jury who don't believe in fossils."

"This can't be happening to me," Homer cried. "Get me out of here, please!"

Janice held his hands tightly and looked into his eyes, "Homer, we will get through this. I will do my best to get you out of here."

The day of Homer's trial was beautiful, climatologically speaking. The South Georgia sky was as blue as blue could be. A few cottony clouds were scattered about, and a cool breeze kept the oppressive humidity on the other side of the Chattahoochee in Alabama.

This being Offbase's first murder trial since Reconstruction, the courtroom was filled to capacity. Outside of the building a crowd of nearly five hundred people gathered. They were certain a short trial followed by a tough sentence of electrocution would be immensely satisfying and would help keep crime away from their town. Several vendors came as well, hoping to catch a little business as a result of the trial's popularity.

When Homer arrived, escorted by Stus and Nancy, the crowd exploded. "Death, death, death to the killer," people chanted.

A smaller group started their own competing chant: "Cute, cute, electrocute!"

Homer, Stus, and Nancy got out of the patrol car just as people started throwing whatever they could grab—popsicles, yogurt, carrot sticks, small rocks, bottles, and plastic spoons. Stus and Nancy tried to shield Homer as they ran into the courthouse.

Inside the courtroom Homer sat down next to Janice. On the evidence table he could see the Cro-Mudgeon Man skull, along with his toiletry kit, and car keys. He also saw some papers and the plastic baggie he had left on his kitchen counter.

"What's that doing here?" he wondered when he saw that last item.

Then in came Judge Ouida Hackett. Though she was small in stature, her terrifying presence was sufficient to silence the courtroom; no gavel was needed. Both prosecutor Buster Jackson and defense attorney Janice Hillmen had, at one time or another, experienced Ouida's ferocious courtroom discipline. Likewise, Bess, Zebulon, Harold, and everyone else in the audience knew all too well the consequences of crossing Judge Ouida Hackett. It was rumored that even mosquitoes feared her blood when it boiled. Everyone sprang to their feet and stood stiffer than the frightened recruits at Fort Blakely.

The judge took her seat, slammed her gavel, and barked at Buster and Janice, "Let's get this over with. Are you two ready?"

"Yes, your honor," they replied.

"Let's hear what you've got. Buster, don't waste my time!"

Visibly shaking, Buster walked to an old lectern with peeling veneer, put on his glasses and began reading his opening arguments. "Your honor, ladies and gentlemen of the jury. . ."

Wham!

Suddenly, in the back of the courtroom, the double doors flung open, violently whacking the walls and then swung back closed. Everyone in the courtroom looked to see who it was. Again, the doors were pushed open, this time a little slower. In the doorway stood what appeared to be a man, peering from beneath long matted hair. He had a wild, untamed beard, and was wearing a Hawaiian shirt and Bermuda shorts that clearly had not seen a washing machine in years. His left arm held a bed roll and in his right hand was a long yellow paper that looked something like a contract.

Janice was the first to recognize him. Pointing at him, she stood up and yelled, "That's Sam Butts!"

Indeed, it was Sam. All over the courtroom you could hear gasps, shrieks, screams, and other noises.

"Judge Hackett, I need to sue somebody!" Sam said in a craggy voice.

Ouida whacked her gavel. "Quiet! Now!" She aimed her anger at the trembling Buster Jackson. "What is going on here?"

The prosecutor's normally nimble mind froze with fear. He replied, sheepishly, "What is going on here, your honor?" This only fueled Judge Hackett's burning temper.

Nancy and Stus looked around for a quiet way to exit the courtroom. Seeing none, they slumped in their chairs, hoping to become less visible.

Ouida slammed her gavel even harder, breaking the handle and sending pieces into the jury box. "Janice, Buster, Sam, Homer, and Stus, in my chambers. Now!"

"Where on God's green earth have you been for the last five years?" Ouida Hackett was sitting at her desk. Her first questions were directed to Sam. "Obviously you weren't murdered."

"No Ma'am," he replied politely. "I thought I was a goner, though." Sam then recounted his long story. "I got a coupon in the mail, Judge, almost six years ago now. It said that if I called this eight hundred number, I'd get a free week in Miami." Sam held up his yellow contract. "This here paper says all I had to do was go to some presentation 'bout time sharin' and vacationing while I was there. And I did, just like they said. But then they wanted a deposit, and seein' I don't got a credit card, they dumped me on the highway and said, 'you can walk back.' Well, Judge, I walked."

"Walk back to where?" Judge Hackett asked.

"Home," Sam replied.

"From Miami?"

"Yes, Mam." Sam placed the contract on Ouida's desk and continued. "I want to sue 'em, Judge. Breach a' contract!"

Ouida looked at Buster Jackson, "Well? Do you have anything intelligent to add?"

"Do I have anything intelligent to add?" he replied.

Frustrated with the prosecutor, the judge turned to Homer. "Dr. Habilis, there is still the problem of that skull. To whom does it belong?"

"The city of Baden-Baden, your honor. I had thought the skull was floating down the Rhine."

Judge Hackett sat back in her chair and rubbed her forehead. "Now let me get this straight. You thought Sam's head was floating down a river in Germany."

"That's not a skull your honor," Janice said, trying to add clarity. "It's a fossil."

Judge Hackett turned to Stus. "Do you have anything to add to this mess?"

"Yes, I do, your honor. There's still that marijuana we discovered in the defendant's kitchen."

Ouida turned back to Homer. "Well?"

"It's oregano, your honor," the anthropologist replied. "I always add some to my pizza."

"Get out of my courtroom all of you, now!" Judge Hackett ordered. "You've wasted enough of my time. Now, get out!"

The following week Dr. Habilis was back on a stage in Baden-Baden for the rescheduled dedication ceremony. Seated with Homer was Mayor Gerhard Hanswurst as well as Heidi Trottelhaus. Stuttgart TV producers were giving the reporter a second chance. Though Attila was safely locked in Gerhard's apartment five blocks away, Homer held tightly to the padded container in his lap. This time he was taking no chances. The mayor was pleased the crowd was back to witness the historic grand entrance of Baden-Baden into world-wide prominence as a center for the study of anthropology.

Over in Gerhard's apartment, seated on a nightstand, Attila noticed that one of the bedroom windows was open. She leapt to the sill, hopped outside onto the roof of an adjacent building, and jumped from building to building until she reached the twelfth century town square. Attila leaped down to the square and then shimmied up a drain spout and entered the second-floor window of Baden-Baden Hall. Trotting onto the stage, she walked to Mayor Hanswurst and hopped into his lap. The crowd froze.

Attila smelled something again. This time it wasn't emanating from Homer. No, the cat picked up the scent of a food product coming from Heidi. The reporter didn't realize that a small piece of carp had fallen into her vest pocket during lunch. Attila did. The cat jumped from Gerhard's lap into Heidi's and buried her head in the reporter's vest pocket.

Heidi screamed; Gerhard turned to Homer and said, "Don't you dare move!" Each person in the audience jumped to his or her feet, ready to flee. The mayor grabbed his cat and held tight. "Homer," he said. "Let's get this over with."

Homer walked to the front of the stage, put the padded container on the presentation table and opened it, removing the prized skull and handed it to the mayor.

Homer never returned to Baden-Baden. He never returned to Germany at all, for that matter. Instead, the professor keeps a low-profile teaching anthropology at Early College.

Officer Augustus C. Bacon could no longer command the fear and respect from the citizens he once so faithfully protected. He left the city and is now the chief of police in Dothan, Alabama. Officer Nancy Jenkins was promoted to the position Stus vacated. Prosecutor Buster Jackson lost his bid for re-election to Janice Hillmen, who was declared hero of the day for securing Homer's freedom. Buster moved to Augusta and now works for a wholesale distributor of corrugated cardboard.

As for Button Gwinnett Benson, he's now mayor of Offbase. Acclaimed by the citizens of Offbase for making a monkey out of the police and the prosecutor, he was the beneficiary of a lot of TV publicity. This former cab driver was elected by a wide margin and is now beginning a four-year term.

When Ken finished his tale everybody aboard the bus cheered.

"I'm touched," he said, holding his hand to his heart. "I thought you'd appreciate my story."

"It wasn't your story that got me cheering," Bob said. The bus was slowing down and getting ready to turn into a huge asphalt parking lot that, save for a rusty golf cart, was empty.

"Lunch is what got us cheering," Jim noted. He pointed to the Thelma's Pit Barbecue sign at the lot's entrance.

"Thanks a lot!" said Ken, feeling a little hurt. After all, he worked very hard on his story.

"Oh, Ken!" Dave said, handing his Bible back to him. "They were just teasing you."

"Understood," Ken replied. "We Lutherans always are the butt of jokes, just look at A Prairie Home Companion."

"We are such a mess," Sarah said. "We leap when we should walk and sit when we should run!"

"I agree," Ron Morgan added. "And we sit a lot!"

"Brothers and sisters, I don't know about you," Dave jumped in, "But I'm famished. Let's get off this bus and eat!"

"We're here just in the nick of time!" Sarah said. "It's too hot on this bus."

"I've been waiting a whole year for some of Thelma's pit barbecue," Jim said excitedly.

"Me, too," Ben, Billy, and Bob said.

"And her sauce," Ken added. "It's so good it's sinful!"

"Her baked beans, too," May said. "They've gotta' real kick to them."

"And the slaw," Sarah added. "Creamy and dreamy!"

Middlelogue

"Dang, it's gone!" Jim cried. "How can it be gone?"

The twelve members of the clergy were standing at the edge of a very large sink hole and looking down at the roof of Thelma's Pit Barbecue, fifty-one feet below. Amazingly, the air-conditioning system, exhaust fans and duct work were still intact and seemed to be operating, though they were rattling a little more than usual.

"Man, oh man!" Jim said. "Swallowed the whole dag-gone building."

"And Thelma's delivery van, too!" Sue said, pointing to the mostly dirt covered truck.

"What'll we do now?" Ben, Billy, and Bob asked.

"We'll have to pick somewhere else to eat," Dave said sadly. "That's what we'll have to do."

"Oh no!" Sue cried. "Not again!" With the lone exception of Princeton, every head was shaking back and forth. Some were even weeping. This being only his first year with the O'Postles, Princeton had not been part of their last ecumenical debate about where to eat.

"What's the problem?" Princeton asked. "There are plenty more restaurants along the highway. Let's just pick one." He was dumbfounded. He could not, for the life of him, understand why choosing another restaurant posed such an insurmountable problem.

"You got any ideas?" Jim challenged Princeton.

"Well, there's that cafeteria right across the street," he suggested with a little incredulity. Princeton thought this simple solution should have been obvious, even to those not well versed in the academics of theoretical group decision-making like Presbyterians were.

"No can do," Sue explained. "We Methodists are boycotting that one."

"She's right," Dave said. "Labor problems."

"Ditto, me," Ron added.

"Okay, how about that sandwich place back at the last traffic light? I could go for some low-fat turkey. They have a vegetarian plate too, and their employees are unionized; they have their own credit union, paid vacation, health insurance, and a 401(k) plan." He thought he had all the bases covered.

"We'd have to wait in the bus," Ben, Billy, and Bob noted. "The Convention's got a problem with some of the magazines they sell."

Princeton scratched his head. He snapped his fingers. "Hey, I've got it! There's a pizza place a half mile up the road. That seems safe enough. I know for a fact they don't sell magazines or even newspapers for that matter."

Ken shook his head. "Count me out," he said. "Their cheese comes from big multi-national corporations. The Synod wants me to support family farms and businesses."

"Well, then," Princeton suggested, getting frustrated. "Why don't we just go to a plain old grocery store and let everyone pick what they want. That way nobody gets left out!"

"Not me," Ed said. "Not if they sell tobacco."

"Or beer," Ben, Billy, and Bob added.

"You see, Princeton, between Columbus and Newnan, Thelma's was the only place we could all eat at with a clear conscience," Dave explained. "Believe me, we've all been down this road before."

"We've been coming to Thelma's for pretty near ten years," Sue said.

Suddenly, a familiar voice was yelling at them from the parking lot. "Don't you go fallin' into that pit!" Dave and the other pastors turned around, looking towards the lot.

"Thelma!" Dave exclaimed. "What happened?"

"Those boys took the limestone right out from under me," Thelma explained. "If the governor doesn't stop those mining companies, one day all of Georgia's gonna sink into one big pit!"

"I'm so sorry," Jim said, offering his condolences. He gave Thelma a gentle hug when she got to the pit's edge. "Do you need us to pray for you?" he asked in his pastoral voice.

"Pray for me? Heck no! I don't need prayers, I need customers!"

"Customers?" Sue asked. "How're you gonna have customers without a restaurant?"

"Why Sue, I'm still open for business." Thelma pointed across the sink hole to a makeshift set of whitewashed wooden stairs leading down to the restaurant.

"You're opened?" Dave was shocked. So was everybody else.

"Floors cracked a bit, but otherwise my restaurant is in fine shape."

"You mean you're still open?" Ed asked.

"How else could I have customers?" Thelma thought the ministers to be a little slow on the uptake. It did take several seconds for the shock to wear off and for the reverends to realize they were going to eat now.

"Praise the Lord!" Nearly everyone said spontaneously. Ken, Sarah, and May clapped their hands. Ed and the trio of Baptists raised theirs in the air while the others smiled vigorously.

"Follow me!" Thelma quickly grabbed Dave's arm and led him to the stairs while, in single file like school children, the other pastors followed close behind.

Reaching the bottom of the sink hole required descending a set of some 197 wooden steps that made a complete lap around the sink hole. With each step, the rickety boards creaked, and some even shook a little. Thelma, however, seemed oblivious to any danger. Dave and his eleven colleagues did their best to be brave; after all, either they followed Thelma, or they had to stay above ground and reach a consensus. The former seemed to be the wiser choice.

When they did finally reach the bottom, Thelma kicked a few rocks out of the way and pushed the door open, and the twelve ministers entered the restaurant.

"The ceiling is a lot lower," Dave noticed. An autographed picture of the governor now had the head cut off, and any customer over six-feet-five now had to duck under the overhead fluorescent lights.

"It's just cosmetic," Thelma explained. "The ceiling frame slipped a bit when we landed. But you know, I was thinkin' 'bout puttin' in a skylight when I get it fixed. We don't get much light through them windows no more." She slapped Dave on the back. "When the peaches fall, you make cobbler."

"Hey, gang," Rex yelled from the steam table. He waved his big ladle in the air. He was really happy to see everyone. "Beans are fresh; couldn't be better; so's the grits."

"Rex, old boy, you doin' okay?" Dave asked.

"I'm fine but Rocky broke his nose on our new milk machine when we hit bottom." Rex pointed to a big dent on the side of the shiny aluminum dispenser. Rocky then stuck his head out from behind the big stove where he was cooking a rack of ribs and waved. His nose was covered in white gauze and surgical tape.

"Wibs, anywudy?" Rocky asked.

"Hey, I don't remember my knees hitting the table," Sarah said. She was the first to slide into one of the booths that lined the walls of the restaurant. Out the window she noticed the roof and part of the windshield of a Volkswagen camper. The rest of the vehicle was buried under dirt and rubble. "You don't think anyone's still in there, do you?" she asked.

"Nah, not unless he had passengers. The owner walked home," Thelma explained. "But his auto insurance company's still jerking him around. Rocky wants to use it for a grease trap, but I told him he's gotta wait to see if the owner comes back."

"Wow, have I gained weight or are these booths a bit tighter now?" Dave noticed, sitting across from Sarah. The table was pressing against his rib cage.

"Sorry 'bout that, Dave. Rex keeps forgettin' his crowbar. I promise, when y'all come back they'll be pulled apart some more."

"We're ready for ribs!" Billy, Ben, and Bob said in unison. "We're famished." They were seated with Ed at one of the tables, which, Ed noticed, was kept level by means of an old phone book stuck under one of the legs.

"Lost bits of my floor," Thelma told them. "But I wanna make sure we don't sink more before I get it fixed."

"That's okay, Thelma," Ed replied. "The table works just fine."

"And it sure beats arguing about eating someplace else," May told her colleagues.

"You know, this place makes me feel like those early Christians," Ron said.

"How so?" asked Dave, surprised at the analogy.

"Remember? They had to worship underground, you know, in Roman sewers."

"Catacombs," Ken said, correcting him. "They worshiped in catacombs, not sewers."

"They were still underground, though, right?"

"Well, yeah."

"This place makes me feel more rooted," Ron explained. "Closer to those early Christians."

"Thelma's is historic. There's no place else like it; never has been and never will be," Dave added.

"Keep the history," Ed said. "I want my ribs."

"Yeah," the trio agreed. "We're hungry."

"Speaking of history," Sue said. "After lunch, I'd like to hear from Bob. He obviously knows much about history."

"Okay, when we're finished lunch and back on earth, I'll go next."

"Can you give us a preview?" Dave asked.

"Finding abundant life," Bob replied. "That's what I have to share with you all."

"Speaking of abundance," Princeton said. "I'll have to try these fried green things."

"Urp."

Rev. Princeton Newport was belching uncontrollably, albeit quietly and under his breath. "Presbyterians do not burp," his mother had often told him as a young lad, and so Princeton was doing his best to keep his indigestion covert. He and the other eleven Early County ministers had finished with lunch and were back aboard the bus, anxious to resume their pilgrimage.

"Urp."

"Princeton, lunch didn't settle well?" Dave asked.

"Urp." Mortified, Princeton could not stop himself. "Urp."

"Is Princeton sick?" Sarah asked.

"What's wrong with Princeton?" Ron wanted to know. "He didn't eat those fried green jalapenos, did he?"

"Urp."

"He thought they were tomatoes," Dave explained. "And he had quite a few, I might add."

"Urp."

"Tomatoes?" Jim asked. "What made him think they were tomatoes?"

"I guess our over-educated clergyperson 'don't know much biology,'" Ron said snickering.

"Somebody get him something!" Sue Moyers said with some urgency. "His face is turning red!"

"Ah, he's just humiliated," May said. "He did the same thing at General Assembly last year."

Suddenly the bus lurched forward, and the twelve Early County ministers were once again on their way to Camp Candleberry, on Summerville's north side. Baptist pastor Bob Bending was working his way to the front row.

"West of Eden," Bob said. "Is the name of my story and a text from the tenth chapter of John's Gospel is what I shall illustrate."

West of Eden

The thief cometh not, but for to steal, and to kill, and to destroy:
I am come that they might have life, and that they have it more
abundantly.

(JOHN 10:10 KJV)

A LOT OF BEAUTY is packed into little Vermont. To some old-timers, the
heart of it all lies due east of the Cold Hollow Mountains, a sparsely populated area dotted with picturesque towns like Eden, Eden Mills, and Eden
Junction. Many of the roads are closed during the winter, limiting access
to these villages to all but the hardiest of travelers. About eleven miles due
west of Eden, at the end of a long straight, and narrow dirt lane, you will
find a small, hand-carved, and weathered wooden sign that simply reads,
Peace be unto you. This marks the entrance to the old Quoter community,
a group of families bound together by their deep faith in God and by their
two-century tradition of keeping to themselves. The Quoters, not as famous
as their Shaker cousins, call themselves "The United Society of Steadfast
Believers in Christ's Second Appearing" and make their gentle living farm-
ing in the foothills of Cold Hollow.

The name Quoters was coined by Horace Greeley in an editorial he
wrote for the *New York Tribune* back in 1843. It refers to what he thought
was an odd habit of this group constantly reciting Bible verses to those
outside their community. But this was not just a habit, it was their way of

keeping the world at bay during that time of arduous and temptation-filled waiting for the Lord's return. While adherents were free to communicate with outsiders, they could only do so by quoting directly from the King James version of the Bible. Their Shaker cousins, in contrast, allowed members to talk with nonbelievers using regular English. By Quoter standards, this was being a bit too comfortable with the world. Unwilling to compromise their faith, the Quoters went their own way and settled in the foothills of Cold Hollow, west of Eden.

Sadly, the twentieth century was not kind to The United Society of Steadfast Believers in Christ's Second Appearing. Expecting the world to end momentarily, more than a few earnest and good-hearted folks had sold their possessions and moved to Cold Hollow for what they thought would be a short wait. But because Jesus failed to reappear by 1899, as their founder and spiritual pilot Mary Lee had predicted, the community started the brand-new century feeling a little less certain of the future. On New Year's Day in 1901, Sarah Smylie, who succeeded Mary Lee as spiritual pilot, spent the better part of the day searching for errors in the original calculations made some seventy-five years earlier. Sarah discovered that Mary Lee had failed to account for leap years going all the way back to the time of King Hezekiah.

"A miscalculation I have discovered," she declared with great confidence the following Sunday. "Before the sun sets on that last day of 1999, our Lord in Cold Hollow we shall see."

Sarah Smylie died in 1951 and left the community an instruction-packed last will and testament, which she had hoped would bring the Quoters out of the eighteenth century, through the nineteenth, and well on their way into the twentieth. A majority of the changes, such as allowing men to wear boxer shorts and permitting the use of buttons and zippers on clothing, were relatively inconsequential. Three were not: Sarah scrapped the office of spiritual pilot and replaced it with a group of elders (to be elected by the whole community); she discontinued the practice of celibacy (provided marriage was an act of faith and not a compulsion of the flesh); and she directed the community to purchase a new Plymouth station wagon (their first, and to date only, car).

"Ahem." Rebekah Riley, a faint-voiced and slimsy elder, called the council meeting to order. It was New Year's Day 2000. "Sisters and brothers, 1999 hath passed. Nay, our Lord didst not return." Inside the stark, white-washed meeting room, around a well-worn rectangular knotty pine table, she and a cadre of long-faced elders and congregants sat in stiff ladder-back chairs.

"Me thinks it wise to refrain from re-tabulating the arithmetic of our ancestors," Elder Leah Shoemaker said. "Doth not Scripture say our Lord shall be likened unto a thief in the night?"

"Aye, sister," Elder Enoch Tanner added. "Ye know not the day nor the hour when our Lord shall appear. With great patience we must continue this wait of ours."

"But Enoch, that is all we have been doing," Elder Ruth Hawkins said with a hint of frustration in her voice. "Soon in Cold Hollow a soul among us there will not be."

"Sisters, brothers, we must evangelize," Rebekah declared, gently. Hush filled the room as each Elder looked at Rebekah, then at each other, and then back at Rebekah.

"Evangelize?" Enoch said, clearly upset. "Sister Rebekah, that would draw us from Cold Hollow!"

Rebekah continued, "It has been well-nigh ten score years since our last missionary effort. It is time once again to reach beyond our hollow."

"Let us not rush, brothers and sisters." Elder Abraham Hawkins was also alarmed. "We've only just donned buttons and zippers. The community might think this too much too soon."

"Aye, Brother Abraham," Elder Levi Cooper said. "I, too, believe our community will think it too much. Away from the fold we might scare them."

"My heart is with thee, Levi," Rebekah said, softly but firmly. "But Brother, everyone already hath left, impatient for the day of our Lord's return. Aside from this Council of Elders there are not seven families among us, most members in their dotage. Methinks we need not worry about more leaving."

"Aye, Sister, Sarah and I are in one accord with thee." Ruth looked to Enoch, Abraham, and then to Levi while Sarah Riley nodded her head in agreement. "When from this earth we depart, no more will there be to carry the light of our witness. A household to join us we must find, one that hath youth and vigor."

"What should we then do?" asked Brother Levi.

Sister Rebekah had anticipated his question. "We shall send one family into the world. They will bring back a new family for Cold Hollow. The harvest is ripe. Our Lord will provide."

"Where should this family go?" Levi asked.

Rebekah had anticipated this question too. She pinned an old map of the eastern United States to a wall. Picking up a wooden pointer, she poked at Inman Park, deep inside the sprawling Atlanta metropolitan area. She turned around and faced her fellow elders. "Brother Seth hath reported unto me that this be among the oldest planned communities of the Outsiders." Elder Seth Riley raised his handwritten report in the air, shaking it a little. Rebekah continued, "As we live in community, people there must likewise live. They will receive us."

"It is distant from our hollow," Levi observed.

"That is why we must choose Inman Park," Rebekah countered. "Methinks the word of the Lord hath not been visited upon these people, for they are too far south."

"And whom shall we send?" Abraham inquired.

Ruth stood up. "Might I suggest Hannah and Jacob? They are young and strong, only in their fifth decade of life."

Sarah clapped her hands in excitement. "Yes, a good choice, Sister!"

"Aye," Levi affirmed. "Hannah is wise, and her character is strong. She knoweth our Plymouth, and its oil she can change!"

"I agree," said Rebekah. "Hannah is a good choice. And our Jacob too. He is, well, um, um, Jacob is. . ."

". . .a nice man," Seth jumped in. "He cometh from good stock and hath a gentle heart."

Rebekah looked around the knotty pine table "We are of one accord, then," she said. Abraham, Sarah, Seth, Levi, Ruth, and Enoch all nodded their heads. "We shall send Hannah and Jacob. They shall go to Inman Park in Georgia."

"What on earth?" Charlie Roberts said to himself. He was watching a brown 1951 Plymouth station wagon with Vermont tags pull into his full-service gas station outside of Perth Amboy, New Jersey. The car was stuffed with pots, pans, clothing, and other house wares. He walked up to the car and peered in the window. The driver, an oddly dressed woman, was holding a large black Bible in her lap.

"Fill ye up then the measure of your fathers. Matthew 23:32," Hannah told Charlie. She stuck her head and arm out the window and pointed to the gas pump.

Charlie stared at the Quoter for a moment before responding. Something about her made him feel kind of warm inside. "I'll fill her up, Ma'am." Walking to the gas pump, he began singing to himself, "Zippity Do-dah. . ."

Jacob, seated next to Hannah, held a big exhaustive concordance in his lap. It was opened to the page containing all the verses using the word *fill*. "Whew," he said to Hannah. "I was sore of heart for well-nigh two hours over this transaction. Methinks we made a fair impression."

"Find something of relation to *payment*, with haste," Hannah told her husband. Jacob quickly flipped through the pages of his dog-earned concordance.

"That'll be fifteen twenty-seven, ma'am." Charlie was back at Hannah's window holding his hand out and smiling.

Hannah gave him a twenty. "Restore the overplus. Leviticus 25:27."

"Thank you, Ma'am," Charlie said, giving the change to Hannah. He walked back to his chair and sat down.

"What are you smilin' about?" asked Duane, a co-worker. "I thought you were all worn out?"

"I dunno," Charlie replied. He looked up at the brown urban sky. "Boy, it's a beautiful day, isn't it? By the way, I'll help you drop your transmission tonight," he said, something Duane thought Charlie would never do.

After four days of driving, Hannah and Jacob had made it to Gastonia, a North Carolina border town wholly dependent upon the traffic its exit ramps could entice off the interstate.

"Our food is gone, and I have hunger," Jacob said respectfully, trying not to sound like he was complaining. It was lunch time and the five baskets of produce and dried meats they had brought with them from Cold Hollow were now empty.

"Husband, our Plymouth we must stop, and nourishment find we must," Hannah said. Seeing a restaurant sign, she steered the car to the exit ramp and then off the highway. She drove through two traffic lights and found what she hoped was a place to eat. The sign read, "Rock & Roll Café."

Do the rolls have stones in them, husband?"

"Rocks and rolls?" Jacob was nervous.

The Quoters sat quietly in their Plymouth for nearly an hour before venturing into the cafe. Hannah tried to peer through its foggy glass door covered with peeling credit card stickers; and Jacob was captivated by the maze of rusty duct work that sat on the restaurant's flat roof.

"I hope we here can sup," Hannah said, a little unconvinced.

They said a brief prayer together and then entered the diner.

Julie thought she had seen every type of customer there was in her twelve years at the diner—police, truckers, farmers, salesmen, felons, politicians, and preachers. Yet, the odd couple seated at booth 14 was indeed very different.

"Can I get you somthin' to drink while you look at the menu?" she asked.

"Peace be to thee. 3 John 14," Hannah said. She and Jacob smiled at Julie. Hannah flipped through the pages of her Bible. Stopping at Proverbs, she read, "Running waters out of thine own well. Proverbs 5:15."

At first Julie felt this answer was weird, but after looking at the Quoters, she felt her mood change. She found their presence soothing. Now smiling, Julie asked them, "You want water?"

"Thy lips speak right things. Proverbs 23:16," Hannah replied, returning the smile.

"Okay, water it is. I'll be right back." She walked to the lunch counter. "Fred," she said softly, not wanting to be overheard. "What's with this couple at booth 14? You ever seen 'em before?" She briefly pointed to Hannah and Jacob seated on the other side of the diner.

Fred, owner and cook, looked at the Quoters. From a distance Hannah and Jacob appeared a bit like an Amish couple from Lancaster. "Ain't seen 'em before. They worry you?"

"Gosh, no," she said, taking a tray with water glasses. "They're just really odd." Julie went back to the Quoters and placed the water on their table. "Now, what can I get you two?" she asked.

Hannah pointed to the picture of Salisbury steak on the color menu and then read from her Bible. "Make me savory meat such as I love and bring it to me. Genesis 27:4." She pointed to the picture of fried catfish and repeated a text from the Gospel of Matthew, "He ask a fish."

"Matthew 7:10," Jacob said to Julie.

"Okay, I take it you want the Salisbury Steak Plate and the Fried Catfish Plate."

"Shall the rock be removed out?" Jacob asked. "Job 18:4.

Julie didn't know how to respond and returned to the counter, handing the order to Fred.

Ten minutes later the Salisbury steak and fried catfish were on the table at booth 14, and the odd couple from Cold Hollow, west of Eden, were enjoying their meal quietly. Julie watched them from a distance for a minute and then took her break. She went to a phone and called her sister from whom she had been estranged for nearly three years, something she thought she would never do.

It took Hannah and Jacob two more days to reach Inman Park in Georgia—one day to get to Atlanta and another day to find the neighborhood in the metropolitan area's chaotic maze of avenues and expressways.

"Fields to plow dost thou see?" Jacob asked anxiously as the couple slowly drove along the tree-lined streets.

"Barns, livestock, chickens, I see not." Hannah, too, was getting concerned.

It would have been impossible for the Quoters to know that while Inman Park was a planned community back in 1888, today it was nothing more than a densely populated urban Atlanta residential neighborhood. It being a Sunday afternoon, they had to drive a while before encountering any people since most were inside watching football.

"There is no land to work," Jacob observed.

"How can this be community?" Hannah was feeling worried.

"Shall we here park?"

"Yes, Jacob, here we shall park." Hannah pulled to the curb in front of a red-brick Victorian style house with a well-nourished lawn where teenager Leoretta Decklebaum was planting some mums alongside the driveway. "If lodging we find not, our Plymouth must serve us another night," Jacob said.

Jacob got out of the car while Hannah remained in the driver's seat, holding the Bible in her lap. It was opened to the book of Genesis.

Jacob walked up the driveway to the teenager and repeated the verse he memorized, "Whose daughter art thou? Tell me, I pray thee: is there room in thy father's house for us to lodge in? Genesis 24:23." Hannah anxiously watched from the Plymouth.

Leoretta stood up and brushed the dirt from her shirt and pants. At first, she was taken aback. You don't see Quoters in this part of the country, not even in pictures. While she quickly realized the couple was odd, she also knew they were not threatening.

"Run that by me again?" she asked, feeling safe and even a little warm inside.

"Whose daughter art thou? Tell me, I pray thee: is there room in thy father's house for us to lodge in? Genesis 24:23," Jacob repeated.

"Dad," she called out. "Can you come here?"

Leo Decklebaum, a muscular Army captain, had been clipping stray blades of grass along his eight-foot privacy fence. He quickly came to his daughter's side.

"I think you better move on. . ." Leo started to say, but the Quoter's gentle presence disarmed him. He stared at Jacob. He then wiped his dirty hands on his clean, starched t-shirt, something he had never done before, and reached out to shake Jacob's hand. "Hi. I'm Leo. How can I help you?"

"You did what?" Alice Decklebaum, a loan officer with Atlanta's Empire Bank, asked her husband with obvious anger.

"I invited them to stay with us."

"Are you a fool? You don't even know them." Alice was furious. "They're perfect strangers! You've left me no time to check their credit score."

"It seemed the right thing to do. Anyway, they're in the living room waiting. Remember, they're a little odd."

Leo dragged a reluctant and nervous Alice out of the kitchen and into the living room to meet the two Quoters. Much to their surprise, Chopper, the family's abnormally large, usually aggressive, Schnauzer, had arrived first and was lying at Hannah's feet enjoying a gentle tummy rub. Chopper was wagging his tail, something Leo and Alice had thought their dog would never do.

"How did he get in here?" Alice whispered to her husband.

"I dunno. I must've left the basement door open," Leo replied. "I can't believe he hasn't bitten her hand off." Then, to Hannah and Jacob, he said, "This is my wife, Alice. We've also have two teenagers. You've met Leoretta. Leo Jr.'s off somewhere watching the game. You'll meet him later."

Alice smiled graciously and took their hands. "Welcome to our home." Like Leo and her daughter, she immediately felt the warmth that emanated from the Quoters.

Hannah and Jacob referenced greetings from a New Testament epistle and then stood silently. Hannah had left her Bible in the car and without scripture in hand, neither she nor her husband could think of anything to else quote in the present situation.

Everyone smiled at each other for a minute or two before Alice finally said something. "Well, I guess I'll finish getting dinner ready. Do let me know if there is anything you need." She left Leo in the living room with the Quoters and returned to the kitchen feeling strangely warmed.

"I wish I knew what to call you two," Leo said. He was still feeling a bit awkward around the Quoters.

If Hannah or Jacob had a Bible, they would have pointed to the verses in Old Testament books of Samuel and Genesis where their names appear. Instead, they continued smiling, feeling like visitors from a distant universe.

"Well," Leo said abruptly, clapping his hands once. "Why don't I show you the guest room?"

He led the Quoters upstairs and down a long-carpeted hallway decorated with photographs and mementos from Alice's and Leo's successful careers. Chopper followed close behind. Leo stopped and proudly pointed to the first picture. "Look at this," he said smiling. "This is me when I first joined up." A gaunt young man with a buzz cut stood awkwardly at attention and looked out from the fifteen-year-old picture. "And look here, you'll love this—my medals." Leo was very proud of his military decorations. "This is my sword. This is my first machine-gun, my M-16; up there's my survival knife and, oh, yes! You'll really love this one, Alice's first hundred-dollar bill. It's still uncirculated!"

The sight of so many weapons made the Quoters shudder for they, like their Shaker cousins, had always been not a little uncomfortable with warfare. As a matter of fact, the last weapon either of them had encountered was a water-logged eighteenth century flintlock that Hannah found when she rescued their cat Jonah from an old well seven years ago. In any event, Leo was oblivious to their discomfort.

At the hallway's end was the guest bedroom where they were to stay. It was bright and spotlessly clean, and the late-afternoon sun was shining through several large windows. Inside was a queen-sized bed covered with a quilt, made of surplus pup tents and two nightstands Leo had constructed using old safety deposit boxes from a downtown branch that Alice's bank had closed.

"You'll bunk here," Leo instructed, trying to sound gracious. "I hope it's comfortable." Chopper followed everyone into the room and licked Hannah's hand. "Boy, I don't think he's ever taken to anyone like this; it's absolutely amazing," Leo said, shaking his head. "Well, why don't you R and R. I'll come get you when the chow's ready."

Leo closed the door and headed for the kitchen to help his wife, something she had always thought he was incapable of doing.

"They don't say much," Alice told Leo, wondering why he was coming into the kitchen, but choosing not to ask.

"I know, all they do is quote the Bible," Leo said.

"They must be Christians, then. Don't you think so?"

"I guess so. But they're not like us. They can't be Baptist."

"They must be Catholic," Alice speculated. "You know, Catholics are so secretive and have all those rules."

"But Catholics don't dress like they do. I'll bet they're Lutheran missionaries. We don't get many Lutherans down here."

Alice leaned against the counter and wiped her hands on her apron. "Never in my life have I met anyone so gentle. It's unnerving."

"Definitely not the soldier type," Leo said. "They must be here for a reason. Maybe God's led 'em to us. Maybe there's something we're supposed to teach them."

Alice pondered Leo's last comment for a moment before responding. "I guess that's possible," she said, still feeling a little unconvinced. "Like you said, though, they're a little odd."

While Alice and Leo were in the kitchen fixing dinner, Hannah and Jacob were lying down on the guest room bed, looking up at a ceiling fan Leo had made from Vietnam-era raft paddles.

"Wife, why hath the Lord brought us unto this house?" Jacob was ill at ease and wanted very much to return to Cold Hollow.

Tenderly, Hannah took his hand in hers. "Husband, I believe this family is the one."

Jacob sat up suddenly and looked at his wife. "This family?" He asked with disbelief. "They are so unlike us. No Christian have we encountered that would keep such armaments nor worship mammon so. Maybe they are Baptists, or perhaps they be Catholic and Romanish at heart."

"Methinks not, husband. Catholics nigh unto Cold Hollow dress not like this family."

"Then Lutheran they must be. Not many find their way west of Eden."

"Jacob, let thy heart be at peace. Me thinks God hath led us to this family. It was foreordained."

"But how shall they learn the ways of our community?"

"Husband, rememberest thou the words of James, 'I will shew thee my faith by my works.'"

"My utmost shall I do to trust in thy judgment," Jacob said, lying back down next to Hannah. "Thou art wise, my beloved." Jacob was now quoting a verse from the Song of Solomon. "As the lily among thorns, so is my love among the daughters."

Hannah smiled and continued the text from memory, "As the apple tree among the trees of the wood, so is my beloved among the sons."

"A sojourn with this family shall it be," Jacob said, still feeling a little unconvinced. "The faith of our forebears we must convince them to come and see. But let us not forget to get the Bible."

A month later, Jacob and Hannah had their first taste of speeds upwards of 80 miles per hour with the windows open. The two Quoters were in the back seat of the Decklebaums' car, squeezed between Chopper and the two teenagers. Jacob was doing his best to hold onto his black broad-brimmed hat, and Hannah, well, she had already lost her bonnet back at the Dundalk exit just south of Baltimore. They were flying up Interstate 95 and were glad to be heading back to Cold Hollow, though they would have preferred to be in the older and much slower Plymouth. While Leo and Alice were both beginning to gravitate towards "voluntary simplicity," the brown station wagon was a little more than they were prepared to handle. And so, they all agreed to leave that car back in Inman Park.

Alice was at the wheel. "I hope you're okay with spending our vacation up there with all the Quoters," she said softly to Leo.

"It's only for two weeks, what could happen?" Leo replied.

"What'll we do there, Mom?" Leoretta moaned.

Leo Jr. was whining. "Can't we go to Orlando? Please!"

Leo turned around and looked at his children. "You'll do just fine," he said. "It'll take some getting used to. I mean no broad band, no cell phones, no streaming, and Wi-Fi. Your mother and I are pretty excited."

"We're gonna die," Leoretta said.

Hannah wanted to offer her perspective on the pleasure of life in Cold Hollow, but every time she tried, the wind that had snatched her bonnet would make a go at the pages of her Bible. Giving up, she thought of her own years as a Quoter teen: barn raisings, gallivanting through the fields and meadows, and crunching on those fabulous sugar-maple chips, the community's seasonal treat now sold in gift shops all over north central Vermont.

Jacob's thoughts were still stuck on Leo's display of weaponry. "Blessed Savior," he prayed. "I hope this is indeed the family for our community."

On the third day Hannah, Jacob, Leo, Alice, Leo Jr., Leoretta, and Chopper turned off County Route 3 and onto the long straight and narrow dirt lane that led to the Quoter community. They passed the *Peace be unto you* sign, headed up a steep hill, and stopped in a clearing shaded by a three-hundred-year-old oak tree and surrounded by five two-story, white-washed brick buildings. At the end opposite the clearing's entrance there was an old iron hand pump and a wooden water trough; otherwise, the area was bare, though very clean.

Leoretta glanced at her brother, "I told you we were gonna die."

"It's so quiet," Leo Jr. muttered. "What happened to all the people?"

Alice turned to her husband. "It's so peaceful," she said.

"We are home, husband," Hannah whispered to Jacob.

Leo removed his sunglasses and was the first to get out of the car. He stood erect, stretched his arms in the air, and looked around as the other passengers climbed out. Rebekah, Leah, Enoch, Ruth, Abraham, Seth, and Levi had watched their arrival from the second-floor window of the third building. After a brief prayer the Quoters came outside and entered the clearing.

Rebekah looked to Hannah and Jacob for some kind of signal of what to say. "Should I quote Scripture? Should I greet them?" Rebekah did not know what to do.

The other elders were accustomed to following Rebekah's lead. Because she remained silent, they remained silent. The truth is, the last time a newcomer had wandered into the clearing was in 1927, and no one back then had thought to record the exact point during the process of conversion that one could actually consider the outsider an actual Quoter. Not Rebekah, nor anyone else in Cold Hollow understood how to tell if and when the Decklebaums would be ready for regular English.

Alice was the first to speak. "The Lord be with you," she said to Rebekah.

Still silent, everyone now looked at Rebekah. The elder walked up to Alice. She smiled, took Alice's hands in hers, and looked deep into her eyes. After several minutes Rebekah finally said, "And the Lord be with thee. Welcome to Cold Hollow. All ours be thine."

Levi, then Sarah, soon followed by Abraham, and finally Leah, Seth, and Enoch reached out to the Decklebaums with greetings in the name of the Lord, warm embraces, and fits of joyful laughter.

"Famished thou must be," Abraham said. "Let us break bread and sup!

What began as a two-week vacation turned into a forty day leave of absence for Alice and Leo. Wanting to extend their vacation a little, their bosses instead felt they required even more time to realign themselves to their employers' values, a need that was becoming increasingly apparent the longer the Quoters remained with the Decklebaum family. During this time in Cold Hollow, Alice, Leo, Leoretta, Leo Jr., and Chopper received a heaping helping of Quoter community life. Alice cherished the time with her family away from foreclosures, asset seizures, and productivity targets. It took Leo all of the two weeks to stop saluting Rebekah. During the third week he started enjoying the fact that nobody was saluting him. Leoretta and Leo Jr. had more time with Mom and Dad in those weeks than they had had during the entire preceding year. And Chopper, well, he loved the absence of fences and the often-dangerous, traffic-filled streets of Inman Park.

"Have you watched the way Chopper runs around here?" Leo said to Alice one evening as they were getting ready for bed. "What a life everyone has here."

"It's not that easy," Alice replied. "These Quoters work very, very hard."

"That's for sure," Leo agreed. "They've as much stress as we do. They have to worry about when the rain comes, if their animals get sick, and a lot more."

"But it's a different kind of worry," Alice countered. "They're not measured and evaluated all the time."

"What do you mean?" Leo asked.

"I have to produce results. If I do, I keep my job. Maybe I'll get promoted. If I don't, they'll fire me. Every month it's the same thing. And look at you. There's always another rank to shoot for. And if you don't make it, they'll force you out at some point, too."

"But that's the way it has to be in the world," he said. "That's how things work."

"I know that, dear," Alice said, climbing into the high, four-poster double bed. She sank deep into the goose down mattress. "I'm not idealizing it here, either," she said. "I know they've got it tough. But at the same time, it's different. They work hard to feed their community. We work hard to climb on top of ours. That's how it's different."

Leo got into the bed and like Alice, sank into the down mattress. He looked at his chapped hands, blistered by the day's use of a hoe. He lay silent for a few minutes thinking about what Alice had said. "I didn't know Leoretta liked ham so much," he blurted.

"Huh?" Alice asked, wondering where her husband's thoughts were going.

"I didn't know Leoretta liked ham," he repeated. "She's fourteen years old, and I didn't know ham was her favorite food. That's pathetic."

"A lot of kids like ham at that age," Alice said.

"But I didn't know," Leo said emphatically. "I was focused on my rank, not my daughter. And I didn't know she liked ham. It's not the ham that's pathetic; it's me."

"Oh," Alice said. She was silent for a few minutes as well. "These weeks away have really got me thinking about things," she finally said.

"Me too," Leo agreed. "Got me thinkin' about a lot of things."

Back in Georgia, with the sabbatical over, Leo attempted a return to his army routine. His first assignment was to attend his division's annual training exercises and mock warfare. Leaving behind spouses, children, and dogs, he and his fellow soldiers headed to a secluded base in South Georgia where they would pretend to shoot each other and try out new attack vehicles. This year's practice combat was directed by General George Armstrong Hornet, a highly decorated and tightly strung veteran of several dozen wars and overseas incursions. Leo's unit was assigned to protect General Hornet, a stress filled 24/7 job that always went to the drawers of the short straw.

"Sir. I've been thinking about some things, Sir." It was lunch time on the third day, and Leo was in the officers' mess tent, seated next to the general and across from the general's aide, Lieutenant Bo Weevil, who was enjoying a bowl of Boston chowder. "Sir. I think we've got too many weapons, Sir. We should get rid of them, Sir"

The feisty old general dropped his fork and looked at Leo. His red face and quivering lip reflected a veritable stew of anger, shock, and confusion.

"Sir. It's all in the Bible, Sir," Leo said.

Lieutenant Weevil started coughing nervously.

"Captain, what bat-brained bunk are you talkin' about?" the general demanded.

Lieutenant Weevil stopped eating his chowder.

"General Hornet, Sir. I really think we don't need so many weapons, sir."

Bo coughed again, and this time a solitary Navy bean shot from his mouth and got stuck on General Hornet's Distinguished Service Pin.

Leo had stayed up late the night before reflecting on a conversation that he had had with Rebekah in Cold Hollow the week before. "Our way is not for all people," she had told him. "Wouldst our Lord have such a thing? This be our daily question." Of weapons she had said, "No such thing didst our Lord carry. No such thing do we." Alone in a tent with his head outside the front opening, Leo gazed at the Milky Way and thought long and hard about her words. Now that he was away from Cold Hollow and in South Georgia with his fellow soldiers, the contrast between these two ways of living, Quoter and soldier, disturbed him greatly.

"Sir," Leo continued to address the increasingly irritated general. "I've been thinking a lot about non-violence, Sir. I think our unit should explore it, Sir."

General Hornet looked at Leo for several seconds and then started laughing. Soon, Lieutenant Bo Weevil was laughing along with every single other officer at their table. Then, the entire officers' mess tent erupted with laughter. When the general stopped, the mess tent fell silent. He looked at Leo and whacked him on the back. "Young man, you're very funny."

"Sir, I am serious, Sir. I believe we should consider not using weapons, Sir."

Bo had thought it safe to start on his chowder again. He was wrong. Another navy bean landed on the general.

General Hornet turned tomato red again and glared at Leo. "This is the United States Army, you fool. Your job is to kill people! Now, how're you gonna do that without weapons?"

Then and there, Leo knew the Army was not for him anymore.

Like Leo, Alice tried to get her personality back into home foreclosures. At Empire Bank, a huge number of foreclosures and asset seizures awaited her.

"Couldn't we give her another chance?" Alice asked. "After all, it's not that the bank can't afford to." Alice was in her division's soundproof conference room, reviewing delinquent loans with her boss and several other loan officers.

"We're foreclosing, Alice," her boss Darnel Lamprey said in a manner that he thought should have cut off any further discussion. "She got her final warning."

"But Sir," Alice continued. "She lost her job when our bank financed that take-over of her employer. She's been in that home for more than fifteen years," she said. "I'm sure if we give her one more month, she will find another job. . ."

Without looking up, Alice's boss cut her off. "Don't make her problem ours. Now let's move on to the next deadbeat."

"I'm not finished, Sir," Alice said, not wanting to drop the subject. Most of the other officers were getting nervous; some wanted to leave the room. A few, however, were happy at the sudden prospect of getting the chance to compete for Alice's job. It came with a corner office, which they sensed she would soon be vacating. "Sir, I've been thinking about some things," she continued.

Mr. Lamprey stared fiercely at Alice. "You have something to say Ms. Decklebaum?"

"I've been doing a lot of thinking, Sir." Alice stood up. Like her husband, she had been reflecting upon the many things she and Rebekah had talked about during the previous forty days. She rested her palms on the conference table and looked at each person in the room. "I think we focus too much on money."

Slowly and deliberately Mr. Lamprey removed his glasses and placed them on top of the meeting agenda. He adjusted the glasses until the top frame was perfectly parallel with the paper's edge. "You've given this a lot of thought, have you?" he asked sarcastically. "And where exactly did you get this idea?"

"Jesus, Sir. He said you can't serve God and money."

"Do I need to remind you that this is a bank?" he asked incredulously. "You're here because of money, Madame."

"I know that. We have a lot, so let's go easy on some of these borrowers. Give 'em another chance. Let's not charge so much interest. Think of the great community we could build here, Sir."

A few of Alice's co-managers were making schematic drawings on their note pads of how they would arrange the furniture in her office. Several others were making pro forma organizational charts that showed how they might be positively affected should she depart from the bank hastily.

"Don't you understand it's not how much money we already have," Mr. Lamprey said, glaring at Alice. "But how much more we can get"

Then and there, Alice knew the bank was not for her anymore.

"What are you doing?" screamed coach Ramsey Blatter. The coach was standing on the sidelines and yelling at Leo, Jr., who he had thought was one of his star players. "What do you think you're doing?" Jumping up and down, Coach Blatter signaled time-out and motioned for his team to come off the field.

Leo, Jr, the starting quarterback, ran to the sidelines with his teammates. Quickly they formed a semicircle in front of their coach and stood silent.

"If I'm not mistaken, Decklebaum, you handed that ball to their tackle."

"Yes Sir, I did," Leo, Jr, said nervously.

"Excuse me," Coach Blatter said to the team. He grabbed the young man's arm and pulled him aside. "Say that again. I don't think I heard you right."

"I said, yes Sir, I did," Leo, Jr, repeated.

"You let 'em have a touchdown, fool!" The coach was trying very hard not to yell at the boy. "Now why would you go and do a dumb thing like that?"

Then, Leo, Jr., shared with Coach Blatter his experience at Cold Hollow and the many things he had learned, especially about being kind to your enemies and about giving you cloak away as well.

"You are a blithering idiot," Coach Blatter said angrily. "The meek don't play football."

Then and there Leo, Jr., knew the football team was not for him anymore.

Leoretta had always been a very competitive member of her school's debate team, that is, until she spent forty days in Cold Hollow. Sarah Bell Kortex, the team's faculty sponsor, was not impressed.

"This is a debate team, young lady." Ms. Kortex was not happy with Leoretta, a student in whom she had invested a lot of her time and debating expertise. "I shouldn't have to remind you why you are here."

"But Thelma was stumped by that last question, Ms. Kortex," Leoretta explained. "She needed help."

"And you thought it was your duty to help her, is that it?"

"Yes Ma'am," Leoretta replied.

"But Thelma's on the other team," Sarah Bell said, unable to understand her student's rationale. She put her hands on Leoretta's shoulders and looked her square in the eye. "When you told her Liechtenstein's head of state, they could've snatched our title!"

"But in Cold Hollow. . ."

"I don't care what they do in Cold Hollow, young lady," Ms. Kortex replied angrily. "You're in Inman Park and this is my team. You can't do that and expect to win!"

Then and there Leoretta realized she didn't want to be on Sarah Bell's debate team anymore.

"Hannah, Jacob, we're back," Alice yelled.

Leo, Alice, Leo, Jr, Leoretta, and Chopper had pulled into the Quoter community's central clearing and were stopped next to the iron hand pump.

"We brought the car," Leo added.

The family got out of the '51 Plymouth wagon as Hannah, Jacob, Rebekah, Abraham, Sarah, Seth, Levi, Ruth, Enoch, and the other Quoters came outside from the various buildings in which they had been working. Hannah and Jacob ran to the Decklebaum family for one large and warm embrace.

"We so much want to stay this time," Alice said with tears streaming down her face.

Levi whispered to Abraham, "Their oil Hannah hath changed," he chuckled.

"No, brother," Abraham countered. "This be the Lord's repair."

Rebekah walked up to Leo and took his hands. "Earlier you were not with us. Now you are," she said to him.

"I don't want to kill."

Alice put her arm around her husband. "And I don't want to take people's homes, Rebekah," she said.

"We're ready for something different," Leo said.

"Abounding in possessions ye will not be," the Quoter told them. "But in life, ye shall."

Abraham spoke up, "Famished thou must be. Let us break bread and sup!"

Rebekah laughed. She whispered to Leo, "It is he who is famished."

Leo, Alice, the teenagers, and Chopper, as well as every Quoter present, headed to the fellowship hall for food and celebration.

And here, in Cold Hollow, west of Eden, the Decklebaum family settled. For them, life would not be easier. No, at times they would encounter tribulations that alone no family could endure. At the same time, however, just as Elder Rebekah had promised, they found something better. They exchanged their old way of living for one that was even older. In so doing, they discovered a wonder-filled abundance one can gain but never acquire.

"West of Eden" thus ended, and Bob took his seat.

"Were you implying that the armed forces are not a place for Christians?" Rev. Ben Boyle asked. "I shouldn't have to remind you that without military might, this nation would not enjoy such God-given abundance."

"Yes!" Billy agreed. "God has blessed this county like no other, ever!"

"One nation under God," Ron added. "No good Methodist would ever question that!"

"Look, don't get yourselves all in a tizzy," Bob said. "I didn't mean to question anybody's patriotism; after all I am Baptist, too. At the same time, I now see things aren't always black and white. We all choose what parts of Scripture we want to follow."

Ben said with a touch of sarcasm, "Nothing's absolute anymore, is that what you're saying?"

"No, no, no," Bob said. "You're not hearing me. It's all a matter of focus." Then Bob stood up and moved next to Rev. Boyle. "Ben, you were a colonel. You served your country proudly." Looking at Rev. Steale, he said, "Ed, you were a successful mortgage broker, at least for a while." Bob turned around and looked at Rev. Moyers, "Sue, aside from family reunions, you're a vegetarian." And finally, to Rev. Newport, he said "Mummy and daddy were very good to you, Princeton. Need I say more?" He returned to his bench seat and sat down, barely avoiding a loose spring in the middle. He continued, "Yet, I dare say none of you would focus on the same parts of the Bible that the Quoters did."

"We've got a big Bible," Ron said. "There's room in it for everybody!"

"Well, not exactly," Bob replied. "What I'm trying to say is that we all see our Bibles in a different light. It's not that the Bible's big enough for everybody. No Ron, I think it's too big for anybody!"

Dave cut in, "Before that great big light in the sky goes out, I think we'd better get our stories moving, okay?"

Ed Steale stood up from his seat. "I'll be next," he declared. "The light that has shined in my heart and led me away from my subprime life," he said. "I once fished for borrowers. Now I am a fisher of people!" Rev. Steale then took his place at the front of the bus. "'Don Key Hoagie of Skidaway,' is the name of my story and my text is from Mark, one with which you all should be familiar; about fishin' for people."

Don Key Hoagie of Skidaway

And Jesus said to them, "Follow me
and I will make you fish for people."

(MARK 1:17 NRSV)

REV. DULCINEA DEL TABASCO, the rector at All Saints Near the Sea Episcopal Church, put down the last page of a fiery sermon. The worshipers, mostly people whose livelihoods were dependent upon fishing and shipping in and around Savannah, Georgia were aghast. In two hundred years no preacher, as far as anyone knew, had ever rocked their boat more than she.

"Well, I did it," Rev. Dulcinea said to herself. She paused for a moment, took a deep breath and continued, "In closing, I'd like to read to you something from the Prophet Amos." Rev. del Tabasco opened her Bible to the text she wanted and read, "The time is surely coming, says the Lord, when the one who plows shall overtake the one who reaps."

Every person in attendance that Sunday morning at All Saints Near the Sea was shocked, if not angered, at what Dulcinea had said.

"It's not my fault the Siberian Jean and Jacket Company uses child labor. What do we have to do with foreign sweat shops, anyway?" a livid Mrs. Cannon asked her husband. "I declare, the nerve of that woman. Just wait 'til I call the bishop tomorrow."

Mr. Jenkins, owner of a freight-forwarding company, grabbed his Bible and Sunday School workbook and marched down the center aisle towards the exit with a clamped jaw and deep scowl on his face. "Who does she think she is?" he grumbled. "We're just a port. Those Siberian jeans and jackets come in container ships. We don't make 'em here; we just unload the ships. I don't come here to listen to that kind of garbage!"

Yes, indeed, everyone was angry. That is, everybody except Don Key Hoagie. He was in love.

On this particular Sunday, Don Key Hoagie sat alone, as was the case last Sunday and each of the Sundays before for most of his life. It's not that he was anti-social. No, most small-time fishermen like Don Key Hoagie sat alone in whatever church they attended, whether it be Presbyterian, Baptist, Catholic, Lutheran, Methodist, or Episcopalian. Like Don, these hardworking men and women wear their trade like a cologne. Near the docks or out on the open seas, the aggressive fishy odor tends to blend in with the surroundings or get dissipated by ocean breezes. But in the closeness of a sanctuary, this eau-de-profession has chased away more milquetoast believers than a summer revival.

Don Key Hoagie, odors and all, was deeply in love with the Rev. Dulcinea del Tabasco. The very first moment she stepped into the pulpit at All Saints Near the Sea, he could see she was unlike any other woman. To Don, Dulcinea moved and spoke with the charisma and authority of an Old Testament prophet. He liked that a lot.

"How will she ever notice me?" he wondered as the angry worshipers cleared the sanctuary. "I'm just a smelly fisherman."

Don Key Hoagie owned a little trawler. He had named it *The Rose and Arnie*, after a favorite aunt and uncle, and he docked it on the Skidaway, one of those small tidal rivers that crisscross the marshy lands just south of Savannah. The little river provided Don and *The Rose and Arnie* with much privacy. Here he could avoid the speeding pleasure-boats of the city's small jet set as well as the snickers and taunts from the more leveraged fisherman with their larger, heavily financed, and technology-stuffed boats.

Built back in 1915 from the remains of a clipper that had run aground on Tybee Island, *The Rose and Arnie* was a simple craft. The engine, while a bit noisy and not at all fast, was strong enough to do exactly what it needed to do. The boat didn't have a computer, Wi-Fi, nor even a DVD player. Don didn't go for that kind of stuff, anyway. Instead, he was happy with his paper charts and the same hand tools his father and grandfather had used. And if he wasn't busy, he'd take a book over a DVD any day.

"She ain't pretty," he'd tell the rare and usually lost tourist that wandered into his part of Savannah. "But I don't have a bank note to pay."

When the sanctuary was free of worshipers, Don Key Hoagie stood up and inched his way along the pew to the center aisle. He walked to the narthex and froze: Rev. Dulcinea del Tabasco was still there. She was talking to Sam Houston Choat, a cousin and confidant of Georgia's infamously popular two-term governor.

"Don!" Rev. Dulcinea said with her customary enthusiasm. She reached her hand out to greet the fisherman.

It suddenly occurred to Don that the logo on the breast of his knit shirt was from one of those companies the Rev. had talked about in her sermon. He covered the label with his left hand and started to reach out to the minister with his right. "Uh. . . Hi, Reverend," Don said nervously. He then realized his pants might likewise have an offending label. Instead of taking Rev. Dulcinea's hand, he reached around to his backside and tried to cover as much as he could with his free hand. "A mighty sood germon Revarund. . . I mean a good rermon Severend," he told her. Don Key Hoagie blushed. Unable to think of anything else to say, he walked sideways to the door, still trying to cover the labels with his hands. He pushed the door open with his hip. "See you wext neek," he said as he walked outside. "You fool," he thought, "That's not the way to impress her."

By 5:00 Monday morning, Don Key Hoagie was on *The Rose and Arnie* chugging up the Skidaway towards Wilmington Island. Under normal circumstances, he would be alert and ready for the day's catch. Today, however, was different. That dreadfully embarrassing encounter with Rev. Dulcinea del Tabasco was the only thing occupying his mind. Distracted, he veered to the port side, not the starboard, and headed up the Wilmington River towards the mighty Savannah. Instead of entering the open seas, he soon found himself smack dab in the middle of the shipping lanes for Georgia's historic port. As he passed Oatland Island, an ocean liner's loud and deep foghorn got his attention.

"What's goin' on?" Looking around he realized he was entering the Savannah River and not the Atlantic Ocean. "Whoa!" he yelled. Don cut the engine, dropped his anchor and brought his little trawler to a halt. He sunk into his captain's chair and watched all kinds of ships pass by on their way to the port terminals. After an hour or so, Don noticed an enormous ship with the name *Iberian Holiday Cruise Line* painted in bold red letters across its black hull.

"Iberian? Isn't that the name of those designer clothes Rev. Dulcinea told us about," he wondered. "It is!" he said. "Boy, they make my blood boil!" At that moment Don exploded. A nitroglycerin concoction of suppressed frustration, internalized humiliation, and unrequited devotion converged and ignited a blast of righteous indignation worthy of the Prophet Amos himself. "That must be the ship bringing them in!" Quickly Don hoisted the anchor and darted to the helm. He revved up the motor and chugged as fast as he could into the wide and mighty Savannah River.

Once in the middle of the river, he jerked the pilot's wheel and turned The *Rose and Arnie* starboard towards Tybee Island and stopped. He cut the engine, dropped the anchor, grabbed his grandfather's megaphone, and moved to the fore of his little trawler.

"Ahoy, there!" Don Key Hoagie yelled into the megaphone as loudly as he could.

High above the Savannah River on the bridge of the *Iberian Holiday Cruise Line* Captain Reginald Winston Coxswald was looking over the seating assignments for the evening's dinner. He was always very picky about which guests of his popular cruise line would have the honor of sitting at the captain's table.

"Captain, Sir." First Officer Alison Berkeley-Jones was holding a pair of binoculars. "We have a small problem."

Captain Coxswald hated interruptions when he was concentrating on seating assignments. "What now, Berkeley-Jones?" he asked with great irritation.

"There's a little trawler blocking our way, Sir. Request permission to stop the liner, Sir."

"Give me those!" The captain grabbed the binoculars to see for himself. "What in the world is he trying to do? Is this some Greenpeace nut?"

About one hundred and fifty yards ahead of the cruise liner, Don Key Hoagie was standing at the very front tip of his boat waving his arms in the air.

"Quick, stop the engines, now!" Captain Coxswald ordered. "Get me the Coast Guard!"

It *took The Iberian Holiday Cruise Line* a little more than a hundred and forty yards to come to a complete stop, but the fearless Don Key Hoagie wouldn't budge. A mere ten yards now separated the tiny *Rose and Arnie* and the enormous cruise liner.

"Ahoy, there!" Don yelled into his megaphone.

Failing to make radio contact, First Officer Alison Berkeley-Jones moved to the fore of the liner and peered over the edge.

"Ahoy, there!" Don yelled.

"Who are you?" Alison yelled back using her battery powered megaphone.

"I'm Don Key Hoagie. My pastor is the most distinguished and beautiful Rev. Dulcinea del Tabasco of All Saints Near the Sea.

"What do you want?" Alison yelled.

"Your pants and coats, you shameless exploiters," Don Key Hoagie replied.

"What did you say?"

"Your pants and coats, every single one of them on your ship. I won't move till you throw them overboard."

"What does he want?" Captain Coxswald radioed from the bridge.

Alison turned towards the bridge and spoke into her two-way radio, "He says he wants everyone on the ship to throw their pants and coats overboard, Sir."

"He what?" the captain yelled back.

"He says we're shameless exploiters, Sir."

"Greenpeace! Darn it all. Not again." Captain Coxswald was fuming. "Did you get the Coast Guard?" he barked at his communications officer.

"They're on their way, Sir," he replied.

"What shall I tell him, Sir?" Alison radioed back.

"Tell him to get out of my way!"

"The captain says, 'Get out of my way!'" Alison shouted down to the fisherman.

"You should be ashamed of yourselves!" Don Key Hoagie shouted.

Meanwhile, back at the All Saints' parsonage, Rev. Dulcinea del Tabasco was watching the end of a soccer match on television. *Terrorist blocks port, details at noon*, a scroll running at the bottom of the screen read. She went to her kitchen, made some tea, and returned to her comfortable chair to watch the midday news.

First, she saw the hundreds of tourists leaning over the railings of *The Iberian Holiday Cruise Line* trying to catch a glimpse of the little trawler that was blocking their way. Behind the liner one could see at least ten or eleven freighters, tankers, and container ships all waiting to enter the port of Savannah. Next, she saw shots of a dozen Coast Guard ships, most with small cannons aimed at a little fishing boat. Then she saw shots of helicopters circling the scene, some from the U.S. Navy, some from the Coast Guard, and some from the local television news stations. Finally, she saw the image of a lone fisherman, standing at the front of a trawler with his hands up in the air, captured by one of the telephoto lenses aboard a helicopter.

"Oh, my word," Rev. Dulcinea said, dropping her cup of tea. "That's Don Key Hoagie!" She put on her shoes, turned off the television, ran to her car and sped to the port of Savannah. "A terrorist? Don?"

Shortly after 1:00 pm, Rev. Dulcinea was down by the riverside. "I can't believe how many news people are here," she thought as she parked her car. Like a herd of single-minded lemmings, every major TV, radio, and newspaper reporter had descended upon Savannah to capture the event. She got out of her car and pushed her way through a maelstrom of commentators, anchors, TV personalities, consulting psychologists, historians, theologians, environmentalists, criminologists, lawyers, travel agents, local celebrities, politicians, and the horde of other experts hired by the media to embellish the human-interest angle of the story.

It didn't take Rev. Dulcinea long to find the person in charge, Coast Guard Captain Lee Ward Leakey, a scruffy man who bore a striking resemblance to Captain Kangaroo.

"What's a pretty little lady like you doin' here?" Captain Leakey asked Rev. Dulcinea.

"I am the rector of All Saints' church," she replied without any attempt to conceal her anger. "That man out there is a member of my congregation!"

"Well, I'm sure he looks a lot like someone in your church, little lady," he said, not believing a word she had told him. "You see, I am an expert on these matters, and what we got here is a terrorist, probably from some foreign country. I certainly doubt we got a church-going American here."

"Why don't you let me talk to him?" she tried to reason. "I think we can get to the bottom of this." She did not vocalize the last part of her sentence, "you twit."

"Little lady, like I said," the captain continued, ignoring her request. "What we got here is a terrorist, could even be French. Now you go on back home. I'm sure there are more important things for you to do there."

After Rev. Dulcinea del Tabasco finished sharing with the captain her thoughts on his attitude, his understanding of the crisis at hand, and his ability to resolve the matter without making it significantly worse (all done with considerable brimstone), she commandeered a small motorboat, persuading two Coast Guard officers to accompany her. She headed across the river while the captain watched sheepishly from the shoreline.

"Don Key Hoagie, what are you doing?" the pastor asked.

The fisherman dropped his arms and faced Rev. Dulcinea del Tabasco. "What am I doing?" he replied.

"Yes, what are you doing?"

"You see that ship?" He pointed to the enormous ocean liner, now a scant three yards away. "It's that Iberian ship with all those pants and jackets made by children you talked about last Sunday. I told them to throw that stuff overboard. I hoped you'd think well of me for doin' this."

Rev. Dulcinea's mind raced through all the possible explanations for Don's current predicament: delusions, dementia, depression, to name a few. She thought to herself, "I don't recall talking about an Iberian. . . Oh no."

"Don't you remember?" Don asked.

Rev. Dulcinea sat down on a bench in the dingy and rested her head in her hands. She then looked up at the nervous fisherman. "Don, dear, I think I said Siberian, not Iberian."

Don looked up at the boat and for the first time noticed the thousands of passengers peering over the side railings. Again, he pointed to the ship, "It's a passenger ship, isn't it?"

"Yes, Don, it's a passenger ship."

"It's not carrying designer jeans and jackets then, is it?"

"Not unless the passengers are wearing them."

Don looked around at the helicopters, the Coast Guard boats, and the line of commercial ships waiting to enter the port. "I'm in trouble, aren't I?"

"I think that would be a safe guess." Her heart went out to the fisherman. Indeed, at that moment he seemed such a pathetic figure. "Don, why don't you let one of these gentlemen help you move your boat to the side of the river so these big ships can pass by, okay?"

"Okay. I think that would be a good thing to do right now," he replied.

Fortunately for Don Key Hoagie, Rev. Dulcinea del Tabasco had another admirer at All Saints Near the Sea: Sam Houston Choat. Unlike most members of the congregation, this one listened to her fiery sermons and thought long and hard about the issues she raised. He knew Don was no threat, let alone a criminal. He also understood that Don was in fact worried about child labor and thought he was doing the right thing. Sam knew he could count on his cousin, the governor, to intervene.

"You have to go easy on this fellow," Sam had pleaded with his cousin, the governor. "We really do need to deal with child labor. He was absolutely right about that. Look, he just got a little mixed up. Go easy on him."

The governor found some spare state property near the port for a new Coast Guard officers' club, and thus the folks with Coast Guard operations in Washington were happy to deal with this unfortunate incident, quietly. Don agreed to some intense counseling and community service work and thus avoided hard labor at one of Georgia's for-profit commercial prisons. Within a few days he was back in his trawler fishing the Atlantic waters off the coast of Georgia.

The following Friday, Sam and Rev. Dulcinea met for lunch at the local Piccadilly Cafeteria. "Sam," the pastor said. "Thank you for saving Don from prison. I don't know what he would have done without you."

"Look, Rev.," he replied. "I understand why he did what he did. And I don't think sending him to prison would have done anyone any good at all. The only thing we need is for him to have a productive life."

"How did you do it?" she asked. "Tell me, how did you get your cousin to fork over that spare property for the officer's club?"

"My cousin is a person of faith. I told him why Don Key Hoagie tried to stop that *Iberian Holiday Cruise Liner* and that God was working in the man's life."

"Sam," Rev. Dulcinea said. "You are truly a fisher of people."

"So are you, Reverend."

"But you were the one who kept Don from drowning in that cesspool of prison life."

"I know," Sam said. "But I had the upper hand."

"What do you mean?" she asked.

"Like I said, my cousin the governor is a person of faith. There are a lot of things for which he has received forgiveness from God, and I reminded him of that. I reminded him that the voters wouldn't be so forgiving if they heard 'bout some of them, especially those dancers from the Cheetah Club. I also reminded him that he was lucky that he had a cousin with such a bad memory."

Later that evening, Don Key Hoagie was in *The Rose and Arnie* chugging towards home after an exhausting day of fishing. In the distance he could see a large container ship out in the ocean heading towards the port of Savannah. He grabbed his grandfather's slightly-out-of-focus telescope to get a better look. On the vessel's hull he could see a name painted in large blue letters. It read *Liberian Shipping Company*.

Don tossed the telescope to the deck and with great force and determination he grabbed the trawler's wheel.

"They should be ashamed of themselves!" he shouted.

He made a quick 180-degree turn and headed back out to sea.

"How dare they!" Don Key Hoagie yelled. "How dare they!"

"Fishing for people is a lot more than passing out tracts or doing alter calls. While Don Key Hoagie's fishing was influenced by a crush on his pastor, his concern for the oppressed shined through. Don, however, should have included his church and elders when he goes after evil. We are not lone rangers," Ed concluded, taking his seat.

"Let me be next, please!" Jim Mayer said with enthusiasm. "What my independent friend and colleague says is true; we must always first be fishers of people. But that's not where it should end!"

"Well, go on then, you're next." Dave said, nervously wondering what was coming.

"It's not enough to just fish for people when our temples themselves are filled with greedy moneychangers!" Jim explained, as he walked to the front of the bus.

"What on earth do you mean?" Dave asked.

"I'll let my story explain what I mean," Jim replied. "It takes as its text verses from the nineteenth chapter of Luke. Verses forty-five and six to be exact. Don't you remember when Jesus forcefully chased the moneychangers out of the temple?" Jim made eye contact with each person on the bus and then read his text: "My house shall be a house of prayer, but you have made it a den of robbers." He closed his thick, index-tabbed, multi-translation, annotated study Bible and dropped it on the vacant front seat. "I'm afraid we've opened the floodgates for them in our own day."

"Go on," Dave begged. "Let's have your story."

"I call my tale, 'Take My Yolk Upon You.' Here it begins."

Take My Yolk Upon You

Then he entered the temple and began to drive out those who were selling things there; and he said "It is written, 'My house shall be a house of prayer;' but you have made it a den of robbers."

(LUKE 19:45–46 NRSV)

"MARY, THE NUMBERS!" SEAN B. Simonie barked as he glanced at his overpriced wristwatch. Sean was President, Chair, and C.E.O. of the Bible Corporation of America, the world's biggest and most aggressive scripture publisher and distributor of Christian widgets.

"Yes, I have them right here," replied Mary Daniel. At thirty-five Mary was not only the youngest division manager for marketing and strategic positioning in the history of the corporation, but she was also the first woman to have this critical role.

"Well? Get on with it!" Sean hated to waste time, even that tiny increment expended on useless eye contact. As a matter of fact, he once rode the elevator twenty-two floors to his office suite with no one other than Mary and did not know she was there.

"Sales of our North American Standardized Translation are down 15.987 percent over the same period last year," Mary reported. She switched on a computer graphics program that projected pie charts onto the wall. "Gentlemen and ladies, each wedge represents an edition of our market-targeted study Bibles. Wedge one is the *Businessman's Bottom-Line Bible*, wedge two is our *Master Chef's Filet of Soul Study Bible*, and so on." She highlighted each product with a laser pointer as she went along.

Mr. Simonie walked up to the projected graph to get a better look. "We lost money on that *Extreme Study Bible for Outdoor Adventurers*. I hate losing money." He turned around and zeroed in on a nervous John Flynch, Division Manager for Product Development. "John, that wedge was your idea."

"Yes, Sir." Sweat was dripping off his nose and running down his back. "We had excellent positives from our focus group. I think it just needs a little more time."

"John, time is something your wedge doesn't have."

"Sir?"

"Our competition is on our heels every day. When our Bibles sell, we make money. When our Bibles don't sell, we don't make money. It's that simple." Mr. Simonie then spoke to everyone at the conference table. "Look, this is a basic biblical principle," he said in a manner indicating that any person who didn't understand was a fool. "Our fruit is profit. We trim those branches that don't bear fruit just like Jesus said to do." He looked back at John. "Prune it!" Every eye followed the president as he returned to his seat at the head of the long, polished-marble table.

Mary continued with her presentation. "We're still on top in terms of overall market share."

"And what's our market share now?" Mr. Simonie asked, fiddling with his financial calculator.

"We hold 37.23 percent of the non-King-James market, sir."

"Our closest competitor, is it still that Transworld Bible Society?"

"Yes, sir. They're at around 35.092 percent now for the same segment."

The president leaned back in his chair and looked up at the ceiling for a second. After scratching his nose, he looked back at his calculator and continued to question Mary. "Last quarter they were below thirty. What happened?"

"They came out with a new translation, Sir. I understand it's even popular with the unchurched market, particularly first-time Bible buyers."

"Doggonit!" the president exclaimed, slamming his fist on the table. "That's not good news. What's wrong with our Bible?"

"In a month it'll be thirty years old, Sir," Mary replied calmly.

"Sir." John Flynch raised his hand and shook it eagerly.

"Yes, John," Mr. Simonie said, authorizing the division manager to speak.

"Sir, I think we could add another study Bible to our product line. Give me a week with my staff, and we'll wedge out another subset of the population. We've been testing a special limited-edition Bullet-Point Bible for busy suburban moms and dads. It's got the whole gospel of John down to seven strategic points! In fact, the whole thing is 93 percent shorter than the old Reader's Digest condensed version."

"Mr. President, may I say something?" asked Robert Beardless, Division Manager for Press Operations and Publishing. Mr. Simonie pointed in Robert's direction and nodded his head. "Sir," Robert continued, "We are working on a new line of covers." Robert reached into his tall sheepskin attaché case and pulled out several display boards that had various samples affixed by Velcro. "These are two of the new covers I'm creating." Robert held one of the boards in the air. "For women we have a new line of faux-mink pink Bible covers. They look expensive, but because they are made in a poor country, they're real cheap to produce. And for men, we've perfected a hard but light weight camouflage metal cover, with an optional logo from a professional sports team."

"Sir, with all due respect to my colleagues, our research indicates people are tired of our North American Standardized Translation. It's been out there for three decades. No matter how we re-package it, we'll still be competing against the newer editions entering the marketplace," Mary said to Mr. Simonie.

"Are you telling me we need to do a whole new version?" the president asked, looking at Mary briefly.

"Well, Sir, it wouldn't hurt," Mary replied. "If dominating the Bible market is your goal, then I don't see any alternative."

Mr. Simonie was silent for a few minutes, thinking about the implications of what Mary had just said. He got up, walked to the window and looked outside. He scratched his nose again and mumbled while his department managers sat perfectly still, waiting to hear his reaction. He returned to his seat and scribbled on a legal pad. "I agree with Mary," he said resolutely. "I want a new version."

"I think that's a wise decision, Mr. Simonie," Mary said.

"We'll take this up at our next meeting. Mary, bring the numbers, what'll it cost us, and how soon can we make a profit. John, bring me new study Bible ideas. I want to divide and attack our markets with surgical precision. Robert, the packaging's gotta be totally new. I want new paper, more pictures, and lush covers." The president paused to give everyone a moment to catch up on their note taking. "I must have everything at our next meeting."

Everybody nodded in agreement.

"Let's move on," Mr. Simonie said trying, to quicken the pace of the meeting. "Bible Derivatives are next. I hope it's good news."

Wilbur Iverson stood up. His legs were shaking. "I have my report, Sir," he said, his voice cracking a little.

"Well, get on with it!"

"Our affinity credit card program with Vulturine National Bank is going quite well, Sir." Taped to the wall was a large graph with a profit line that stretched to the ceiling tiles. Wilbur pointed to it. "And we now have three designs for our *Jesus Paid My Debt* premiere plus platinum credit card." He turned off the lights and flipped on a projector. "Here you can see our newest one. It shows Jesus looking down from heaven at a typical middle-class, majority-population American family kneeling in prayer. I think it'll be quite popular. And with an APR of 32.99 percent, our return will be substantial."

A week later the division managers were back around the polished-marble executive conference table waiting for their president.

"He's gonna flip when he sees how much it'll cost to re-translate the Bible," Mary said. "I'm so nervous, last night I didn't sleep at all."

"God's in control, Mary." Robert was emphatic. "It's wrong to feel like that."

"That's easy for you to say," John replied. "You didn't have to lay off six people when Simonie trashed my *Extreme Study Bible*. I don't know what he's gonna do when he sees Mary's numbers."

"Haven't you ever read Romans 8:28? All things work for the good!" Robert countered. "Like our boss says, we don't need to fret about negative stuff."

"Oh, go jump in a lake, Mr. Sanctimonious," John said, getting snippy.

Robert was about to throw his Bible at John Flynch when Mr. Simonie entered the room. "Good morning," the president bellowed.

Everyone immediately turned toward the doorway at the sound of their leader's commanding voice. "Good morning, Sir," the division managers replied in unison. They stood up and waited for the president to lead them in prayer.

"Colleagues, pray for me while I pray for our corporation." Mr. Simonie bowed his head and prayed. "Creator of all we have, thou hast brought forth tremendous success to our humble but mighty corporation. Thy power hath carried forth our products unto the furthest ends of the earth. For this we give thee thanks. Bless our investors as they have blessed us; keep them sound in thy never-ending liquidity. Amen." Mr. Simonie sat down; his staff did likewise. He pulled his financial calculator from its black leather case and barked at Mary. "Mary, the numbers!"

Mary said a little prayer herself. She stood up and opened her presentation program which was now visible on a large screen attached to a wall. "Sir," she said, her voice cracking a little. "This is a proforma seven-year budget that itemizes costs of translating the Bible." She pointed to a lengthy set of rows and columns projected onto the wall. "We have salaries, payroll taxes, benefits, travel costs, reproduction, fees to various universities and seminaries, editorial expenses, computers, programs, interns, miscellaneous. . ."

"Mary," Mr. Simonie snapped, cutting her off mid-sentence. "What's the bottom-line?"

"$9,000,000 to $11,000,000 dollars and seven years, Sir."

"And you're telling me it'll take seven years?" the president asked.

"Yes, best case scenario."

"Nine to eleven million and seven years," Sean B. Simonie repeated. He smiled at Mary, who then started to relax a little (as did everyone else around the conference table).

"Sir," Mary continued. "I really thought you'd be upset with these numbers."

"Me, upset? No, I'm not upset. You might be, however."

"Sir?"

"I want it ready in seven months. Your budget's capped at $9,000."

All the division managers were stunned. "Sir, I don't think we can do that. It took Transworld Bible Society eight years to prepare a new translation and a lot more than $10 million. Did you really say seven months and $9,000?" Mary was feeling very defeated.

"Was I not clear enough? You heard me right."

The room was perfectly quiet. No one knew what to say or how to respond. The project they would soon have to undertake now seemed downright impossible.

"Look," Mr. Simonie continued. "You are all intelligent and creative people. That's why I pay you. Before I leave here today, we can develop a plan to accomplish the impossible." The corporation president got up and walked to the screen displaying Mary's chart. "It's simple. All we gotta do is cut production steps and add new revenue. Think outside the box!" Mr. Simonie stepped to a marker board and wrote a big number one. "Now give me some ideas."

John Flynch was the first to speak up. "Well, Sir, we could cut out all those maps at the end of our Bibles. That would cut production costs a little. I don't think anyone really uses them anyway."

The president started to write this but stopped when Robert spoke up.

"I've got a better idea Sir." Robert was feeling quite confident. "Maybe the maps themselves could be a source of revenue." Robert grabbed a Bible and held up a map of St. Paul's missionary journeys. "Look at all these ancient towns nobody lives in anymore. Who cares about 'em?" He pointed to the Greek isles. "But I'd be willing to wager some of those resorts in the Aegean would pay a lot of money to get put on our Bible maps in their place."

Mary couldn't believe what she had just heard.

"Great idea, Robert." Mr. Simonie noted the idea on the board. "You're a real thought leader. Okay, number two?"

"Why don't we go ahead and do the same thing with footnotes. We could get companies to plug their products in the margins." John was riding a wave of newfound boldness.

"Excellent idea, John. Let's do it." Mr. Simonie noted this as number two on the list. "Okay, number three."

Mary was speechless.

Robert raised his hand. "Sir, we could get student interns to do the translating. That would save a bundle in payroll and consultant costs."

"Not bad, Robert," the president replied. He stopped for a moment to think. "You know, you just might be on to something. Why do we even need to re-translate the thing anyway?"

"What?" Mary asked incredulously. "I thought you agreed that a new translation was needed?"

"I said we need a new version. Maybe we can do this without translating the thing all over again."

"How would we do that?" John asked, confused.

"Look, the King James version is in the public domain, right? John, you get some English majors from that college near here to just reword the thing, you know, with regular every-day English. I think they'd work for free if we provided a lot of free food and beer. And if we got enough of them, we could whip it out in two months!"

"Then how could we call our Bible a translation?" Mary asked, trying to mask her anger. She could feel the last vestige of her integrity escaping through the office ventilation system.

"Mary, you're not thinking outside the box." Mr. Simonie was very irritated with her. "We'll call it something else."

"Like *rendition*," Robert suggested.

"Exactly," Mr. Simonie said with enthusiasm. "You're a team player." He wrote the word on the board. "What should we call my new Bible? Any ideas? I want something that sounds genuine."

"What about the 'A Rendition for All People?'" Wilbur offered.

"Too liberal sounding," Mr. Simonie replied.

John raised his hand. "Well, how 'bout 'A Christian Rendition for God's People?'"

"Too conservative, too restrictive."

"I know," Robert said. "a Christian Rendition for All People."

"Hell, I like it!" Mr. Simonie said, writing in down and circling it.

"This is a dream," Mary thought. She scribbled the Bible's name on her note pad and shook her head. "I've got to get out of here."

In nine months, the *Christian Rendition for All People* was born into the marketplace, just in time for the humongous Faith-based Book Sellers Convention. This year it was in Atlanta, the Bible Corporation of America's hometown. The event was so important to Mr. Simonie that he forbade all vacation, personal leave, pregnancies, and illnesses. Nothing was to interfere. The president also staffed two full convention booths—one for his new Bible and another for the corporation's line of Christian widgets. This year, besides the *Christian Rendition for All People* the company was introducing a new line of faith-based alarm clocks.

"Mary! It's so good to see you at this convention," Sandra Beeble said.

Dr. Beeble, a well-known biblical scholar, was a professor of New Testament at Free for All Theological Seminary in Conyers, Georgia. Being one of the translators of the Transworld Bible Society's new version, she took a deep interest in biblical scholarship and loved working with the ancient texts.

"Hi, Dr. Beeble," Mary replied, feeling a little uncomfortable at seeing this renowned biblical scholar.

"I'm curious," the professor said. "I never knew you were working on a new version. How did you keep it a secret for so many years?"

"Well, um, um. . . I'm not sure."

"I wasn't aware that any seminary was working with you."

"Actually, the folks we used came from the university community." Mary still could not make eye contact with Dr. Beeble.

"Oh, that's interesting. Well, good luck with it."

"Whew," thought Mary. "That was close."

"Mary! Hello!"

"Hi, Fred," Mary said to the Executive Director of United Sunday Schools of the South. Fred Wellwisher was flipping through a sample copy of the *Christian Rendition for All People.*

"This seems genuinely readable. Could I use it with our Sunday School lesson plans? We need something kids and young people will wanna read. I can't use anything that sounds too scholarly."

"Fred, trust me, I don't think you'll need to worry about that with this Bible."

"I do trust you, Mary; you'd never steer me wrong. I'll use it."

Mary sighed as she watched Fred move on to the next booth. "This isn't right," she said to herself.

"Hey Mary! What's it been, a year? Boy, you look depressed."

"Rocky, how are you?" Rocky Rhodes was the owner of a small chain of Christian bookstores located in Georgia and Alabama. "Last time I saw you was at the Miami Beach convention, two years ago," Mary said.

"This new Bible y'all are putting out, do you think it'll make a good pew Bible? It'd have to be something you could use for liturgy, you know, baptisms, communion, weddings, funerals—stuff like that."

Mary's heart sank at the thought of the *Christian Rendition for All People* being used at her own wedding or funeral, though neither was on the immediate horizon.

"If this Bible sells well, then I'll use it for my own funeral."

"That's good to hear," Rocky replied, mistaking Mary's sarcasm for an endorsement. "I'll put in a big order!" By the time Rocky had briefly looked through the sample Bibles, lunch hour was at hand.

Wilbur was in the company booth for Bible Derivative Products that was adjacent to Mary's and was busy demonstrating some of the company's new alarm clocks. He flipped the switch for a jumbo free-standing electronic cuckoo clock with a relief image of Jesus hugging half a dozen baby chickens. A little plastic hen on a stick emerged from behind a simulated barnyard door and one loud "Cock-a-doodle-do" announced the time: 1:00 pm.

Mary wandered over to Wilbur's booth to see the clock. "That hen sounds more like a rooster to me," she said. Mary then remembered what Jesus had said to Peter, "Before the cock crows today, you will deny me three times." Her mind replayed the conversations she had just had with Sarah, Fred, and Rocky. "I've denied our Lord three times!" she cried.

"Huh?" Wilbur asked. "What's wrong with you?"

Mary was now weeping bitterly.

"I hope you're not having a personal crisis! You know it's not allowed this week!"

Mary looked at Wilbur with disgust. She took a swing at the simulated barnyard door and knocked the little hen off its stick. She then turned and ran from the convention hall, as fast as her feet could go.

"Momma, don't worry, I'm in Birmingham," Mary said into her cell phone.

Mary had checked into a motel that sat alongside Interstate 20, just outside of the Alabama city, and for three days she hid herself from Mr. Simonie, the Bible Corporation of America, Wilbur, and everyone else she knew. On the evening of the third day, she called her mom.

"Why didn't you tell me where you were going?" Her mother asked. "Mr. Simonie has called several times every day. He's really worried about his Bible."

"Momma, I want to be alone."

"Why can't you be alone here? That way I could take care of you."

"I'm just like Peter," Mary said, crying.

"Well, I don't see why. He didn't go to college like you. And besides, he's never held down a job like you, either."

"I'm not talking about my cousin, Momma. I denied our Lord, just like the apostle."

"Oh, that Peter. Are you pregnant?"

"No, Momma. Look, I'm okay. I just need some time to sort things out."

"I still don't see why you can't do that here. You could have your room back. I'll move grandpa's things to the garage. Your old bed and dresser are in the attic. I'll bring them down and set everything up just like it was when you were little. You can sleep here and then in the morning, I'll make you your favorite breakfast, every day. Please."

"Thanks, Momma, but I don't think so. Look, I've gotta go."

"Are you sure you're not pregnant? If you are . . ."

"No! I'll call you later."

Mary put the phone down and got into the bed. On the nightstand next to a small lamp was a Bible, the cover of which had a gold letter imprint reading, "Placed here by the Transworld Bible Society." For the last several days she'd been feeling too guilty to touch it. Finally, Mary took the Bible in her hands and opened it. Whether by chance or design, Mary happened upon the book of Jonah, which she read three times before falling asleep.

The next morning Mary got up early, took a long hot shower, and called her mom once more before checking out of the motel and heading back to Atlanta.

"Momma, I'm going to Nineveh."

"Is that far away, dear?"

"Don't you remember Jonah?"

"Isn't he living in Cedartown with that Rhonda woman? I never liked her. You're not going to stay with him, are you?"

"I'm not talking about Joe, Aunt Narcissus' and Uncle Narcissos' son. I mean Jonah in the Bible, Momma!"

"Oh, your grandpa will be so pleased. He always wanted you to be an archeologist."

"I don't mean literally. I'm going to see Mr. Simonie. I've got to clear my conscience."

"Oh, good, you're gonna ask to get your old job back!"

"I don't think so, Momma."

"What? I'm sure if you'd apologized and took a big cut in pay, he'd let bygones be . . ."

"Momma, you're not listening. He's the one who should feel guilty."

"What about your job security? They had such a nice retirement plan and an employee discount on top of that."

"I don't want their discount. Did I tell you about how we made that new Bible? It's a fraud. I'm not gonna sell it anymore!"

"I'm sure Mr. Simonie didn't mean any harm, dear."

"All he cares about is making money. There's not one single drop of faith in it at all. And Momma, I can't take it anymore. I've spent the last three years in the belly of a whale."

"Maybe Doctor Maladie could prescribe something for you. You always had such trouble digesting green vegetables." Her mother continued, "Mary, of course I remember Jonah. I don't see what it has to do with getting your old job back. All you have to do is to say you're sorry and offer to work at a lower rate for a while."

"Momma, I'm gonna go now. I love you." Mary put down the phone, grabbed her keys and headed out the door. "I wonder what Jonah's mother was like," she thought.

Meanwhile, back in Atlanta, Mr. Simonie and his staff at the Bible Corporation of America were in for an unpleasant surprise. It started with one seven-year-old Freddy Wellwisher, son of United Sunday Schools of the South director, Fred Wellwisher, and a picture the little boy was drawing with crayons in Sunday School.

Sally Anne, his teacher, sat down next to Freddy in one of the kid-sized chairs to watch the young boy hard at work.

"Who's that you're drawing?" she asked.

"That's Jesus, Ma'am," he replied.

"Oh, I see. And what's that yellow stuff on his back?"

"Scrambled eggs."

"Scrambled eggs? Why would Jesus have scrambled eggs on his back?"

"Says so in my Bible."

Sally Anne, a student at Free for All Theological Seminary, thought for a moment. She couldn't recall any reference to scrambled eggs in the Gospels nor anywhere else in the New Testament for that matter.

"I don't think Jesus ever had eggs on his back, Freddy," she said, trying not to sound critical or judgmental. "Where did you get that idea?"

Freddy picked up his copy of the *Christian Rendition for All People* his father had given him and opened to the middle of Matthew's gospel. He then handed the book to his teacher. "Here," he said, pointing to the text.

She read the verse aloud. "Take my yolk upon you and learn all about me." Sally Anne stopped reading. "That can't be right." She looked at the cover of the Bible. "A *Christian Rendition for All People*, where did you get this?"

"My dad gave it to me. It's brand new. He got it at some big meeting he went to."

"Do you mind if I borrow it?" she asked. "I'll bring it back next Sunday. I'd love to have your picture of Jesus, too."

"I guess that's okay. My dad's got a whole box of 'em."

Monday morning Sally Anne stopped by the office of Dr. Beeble, in whose New Testament survey course she was currently enrolled. She knew Dr. Beeble was active in the Bible translator community, and she thought the professor might be able to shed some light on this new version.

"Sally Anne!" Please come in," the professor said, greeting one of her favorite students.

"Hi, Dr. Beeble." Sally, happy to be in an adult-sized chair, sat next to the professor's old desk. "I need to talk to you about something." The student pulled Freddy's picture and the copy of the *Christian Rendition for All People* from her bookbag and handed them to Dr. Beeble. "What do you know about this new version of the Bible? It's filled with mistakes."

"Mistakes, what are you talking about?"

"Since when did Jesus enjoin us to take his yolk upon us?"

"His what?"

"Look at Matthew 11:29."

"Oops," Dr. Beeble said. She shook her head. "Just a typo the editor should have caught." She started to laugh a little. "Is this what that picture's about?"

"Yes. Now read chapter twelve."

"Oh, my word." The professor looked at her student. "This has the disciples eating corn on the cob. Corn is from the Americas! The word corn was used in the King James, but that word meant grain back then."

"And check out the footnote that goes with it. It's about some brand of microwave popcorn."

Dr. Beeble then skimmed through the rest of Matthew's Gospel. Sally Anne watched the normally reserved scholar make increasingly dramatic faces, moving from concern to shock, then to anger, grief, and horror.

"The whole Gospel is like that," the professor said.

"Not just the Gospel, the whole thing!"

"You mean the whole New Testament?"

"I mean the whole Bible! And wait'll you see the maps at the end!"

Mary Daniel didn't notice that Dr. Beeble had just backed out of a parking spot at the Bible Corporation of America. As a matter of fact, the former employee parked her car in the same visitor space that the professor had vacated. Mary had come all the way from Birmingham to see the same man who had received a vehement tongue-lashing from a scholar who had a thorough understanding of ancient Greek, Hebrew, and Aramaic as well as a first-hand familiarity with many of the ancient manuscripts of the Bible. When Mary got to Mr. Simonie's office, the corporation president was kneeling at the side of his executive desk and sobbing uncontrollably. She marched forcefully into Mr. Simonie's office, feeling empowered and ready to speak on behalf of the Holy.

"We should be ashamed," she proclaimed with all boldness. "We've traded our faith for a buck! We should be. . ." Mary stopped the speech she had practiced a thousand times on her long drive to Atlanta when she realized that Mr. Simonie wasn't in his chair.

Mr. Simonie looked at Mary. "I'm a sinner," he said sheepishly.

"Sir?" she asked.

"I'm a complete fraud."

"What are you talking about?"

"Our new Bible, it's been exposed. No one will buy it now."

Mary stared at Mr. Simonie without emotion. His handmade suit and shirt, usually crisp and highly starched, were now wet with tears and wrinkled. He used his silk tie to wipe his nose and eyes.

"If God forgives me, my reputation can be restored," he cried. He looked up at a large painting that hung on the wall to the right of his desk. It depicted an oversized Jesus knocking on the side of a non-descript modern office building. "I'm going to turn things around here. God's gonna come first from now on!" He wiped his eyes again and glanced at Mary. "What do you want?" he asked.

"Oh, nothing," she replied. "I'll see you later."

Mary dashed outside as fast as she could. Before she got to her car, she saw a furious Rocky Rhodes pulling into a visitor's space. Rocky and one of his warehouse workers were in their company pick-up truck hauling several dozen cartons marked *A Christian Rendition for All People* as well as a portable hand-truck. Both men were going to camp in Mr. Simonie's office until every dime Mr. Rhodes had spent on the Bibles was returned, with interest and expenses.

Mary drove clear around Atlanta on the great perimeter highway five times before heading to the Chattahoochee Nature Preserve. She sped through the entrance gate, failing to notice a large "Closed for Maintenance" sign, and stopped her car in the shade of an overgrown clump of privets. She was exceedingly angry, not with Mr. Simonie, nor Wilbur, nor with the Bible Corporation of America, nor even with her mother. Mary was mad at God.

"Thank you very much," she said getting out of her car. She slammed the door "You let that greedy boss off the hook, and now I'm the one who has to go to the unemployment office. I got no job, no health insurance, a car payment, rent that's due, and no money. Thank you, God. Yes, thank you very much!" She kicked her car. "She kicked it again. "I knew it. You always forgive the schmucks, and people like me, who work hard, who do what they're supposed to do, who get egg on their face." Mary slumped to the ground. "At least it's shady here."

The former Bible Corporation of America employee sat motionless and stone-faced for nearly an hour, and then the loud roaring of a chain saw got her attention. The Chattahoochee Nature Preserve maintenance department had finally gotten around to clearing the park of its fast-growing privets. The next thing Mary heard was that crackling sound made by splintering wood and then a loud crash. The largest of the privets that had been providing shade was now resting on her car. She climbed out from beneath a mass of branches and leaves and fell to her knees.

"Lord, just take me now. I don't care anymore!"

"Mary dear, I don't understand why you're so cross with that poor Mr. Simonie. You know he was only looking out for the company and his stockholders." Mary's mother was at the stove cooking a batch of scrambled eggs for breakfast.

"But Momma, we're talking the Bible, the Word of God, the Holy Scripture. At some point you've gotta stand up for something."

"I know, but a lot of people had their livelihoods riding on company sales. And don't forget all those 401(k) plans. Folks need to have somethin' when they retire."

"I know that. But he tried to use Scripture to make a lot of money. That's all he cared about."

"And you thought it was your job to stop him?"

"Dr. Beeble got to him first, but I'm still angry, Momma. Mostly at myself. And Mr. Simonie. And Wilbur. And John and Robert for that matter. We should've known better."

Mary's mother finished cooking the eggs, served them onto the oven-warmed plates, and sat down to eat with her daughter and grandpa. She said a blessing and poured three glasses of freshly squeezed orange juice. "I still think you would've liked having that employee discount."

"Perhaps, Momma, perhaps I would have."

"But you know, Mary, your father would be proud of you. You followed your conscience."

"Not at first. Anyway, I'm glad I got out of there."

"You'll find something soon enough. You remember what Paul said, 'All things work for the good. . .'"

"Let's not go there, okay Momma?" Mary turned to her grandpa. "I think he's trying to say something."

Sitting in the corner, Mary's ninety-three-year-old grandpa had been quietly listening to the conversation. "Scrapple," he grumbled.

"What did he say?" Mary asked.

"I think he said scrapple," Mary's mother replied. "Remember he grew up in Delaware. People eat it up there.

"You heard me," he growled a little louder. "That Bible business is like scrapple. Looks nice n'crisp on the outside when you order it, but inside, it can get disgusting."

"I get the picture, Grandpa," Mary said. She and her mother looked at each other and started laughing.

Meanwhile, back at the Bible Corporation of America, Robert Beardless was at desk reading the old thesaurus he had borrowed from his sister.

"We're saved," he yelled. "Hallelujah!"

Robert got up from his desk, grabbed the book, and ran to see his boss. Excited and determined, he walked past the secretary and went straight into the president's office. A deflated Mr. Simonie was still beside his desk, kneeling in prayer.

"Sir!" Robert said with all the enthusiasm of an evangelist.

"Is that you, Robert?" Mr. Simonie asked.

"Sir," Robert said, kneeling next to his boss. "We are saved!" He opened the thesaurus and pointed to a three-syllable word that he knew would change everything.

Mr. Simonie looked at that little word for a long time. He started feeling re-inflated. He then stood up, tightened his tie, did his best to straighten the wrinkles from his pants and suit jacket, and took a deep breath. "Paraphrase, you say."

"Yes sir!" Robert said proudly. "Let's use paraphrase instead of rendition for the title."

"Paraphrase instead of rendition," Mr. Simonie repeated. "I think it'll work."

When Rev. Mayer finished his tale, he reached down and retrieved his heavy Bible, which by now had sunken deep into the bench's worn cloth covering. What's with scrapple again? Rev. Dave Tucker asked.

"Hey, my niece was in the Little Miss Apple Scrapple Pageant last year," Ron said. "She and her family go to the Apple Scrapple Fest in Bridgeville every year. And she won the skillet toss."

"Apple Scrapple Fest? Bridgeville? What are you talking about?" Dave asked.

"Bridgeville, Delaware. It's a big deal. Her governor even goes."

"Now I'm lost," Rev. Presley said. "What does this have to do with anything?

"Can we go back to the point of the tale. I'm sorry I used the scrapple analogy" Jim was getting annoyed. "Look, I once heard an executive in the Christian book publishing industry say, 'The Bible is the lead product from which all other products are spawned.' This is where my idea came from.'"

"Money changers in the temple," Ron Morgan said.

"You see, we do need our denominations and seminaries," Rev. Presley said. "They protect our members from scoundrels like Mr. Simonie."

"Don't forget our seminaries preserve sound teaching," Princeton added. "And our denominational agencies can screen out the things hucksters peddle!"

"Exactly!" Rev. Mayer continued. "My point to everyone is that just because you don't have a big denominational hierarchy doesn't mean you're really independent. Like a thief in the night, profiteers use their marketing powers to steal our independence away."

"On that note, I'd like to go next," Rev. Boyle said. "It's time you all heard from someone with a prophecy to share!"

Jim returned to his seat. All wondered what prophecy they would hear.

"My prophecy will take us in a different direction," Ben explained. "I'm going to explore a time in the far, far future. But first, let me share with you my text." Rev. Boyle read from his pocket Bible, "'Woe to you who are full now, for you will be hungry.' My tale is called 'APE,' a simple title, but its meaning, you will see, is very complicated."

APE

Woe to you who are full now, for you will be hungry. Woe to you who are laughing now, for you will mourn and weep.

(LUKE 6:25 NRSV)

"WHAT A PERFORMANCE, REV.," Bob Dowdy said to Dick Lacuna, pastor of the First Uni-Clep Church of Rockmart. "Kept me feelin' free and worriless for a whole hour!"

"I appreciate that Bob," Rev. Lacuna replied with a grin. "It took me a while to get comfortable with that APE thing-a-ma-gig. I think it adds a lot to our worship and praise service."

APE, an acronym for Atmospheric Projection Equipment, is a new and still-developing technology, even for people like Bob Dowdy and Rev. Lacuna, both of whom live in the heart of the twenty-fifty century. This quirky and sometimes unreliable device projects a three-dimensional image in the air by using water molecules present in any naturally or artificially humid environment.

The pastor put his arm around Bob Dowdy, a retired mood analyst with the county government. "Hey, you gonna join us downstairs for lunch?"

"Planning to," Bob said eagerly. "I hear they're serving fiber-cubes today. Orange ones, I hope. I love that color."

First Uni-Clep Church of Rockmart is the largest congregation in Georgia. It is connected to a denomination created back in 2135 from the merger of the United Methodist, Roman Catholic (in North America), Lutheran, Episcopalian, and Presbyterian churches. Originally called the United and Semi-Roman Cleperitarians of America, Incorporated, the name was quickly shortened to Uni-Clep since most members found the actual name too long, too difficult to remember, and too unappealing.

Accompanied by the church's newest member Blanche Whyte, Bob Dowdy and Rev. Lacuna headed downstairs to the fellowship hall. Once there the three paid a $666 fee by swooshing their bare elbows back and forth across their chests. They then took their place in line.

"I'll take an orange cube," Blanche told head kitchen volunteer Organique Freet when she got to the counter. Blanch took a five-sided sealed container and waited for Bob and Rev. Lacuna.

"Orange for me, too," Bob said.

"We're out. That lady took the last one," Organique said, pointing at Blanche. "You'll have to take a blue one, Mr. Dowdy."

"But I don't like blue."

"Well, we got a few red cylinders left from last week. Take one of those."

"Nothing orange?" Bob asked, not bothering to hide his disappointment.

"I got some ecru semi-solids. If you squint, they look sort of light orange."

Bob thought for a moment and frowned. "No, I'll just take a blue cube," he said finally. "Thanks anyway."

Rev. Lacuna was next at the counter. "Hey Organique, let me have those cylinders and hold the semi-solids."

Blanche, Bob, and Rev. Lacuna sat down at the nearest table and waited for the pastor's slightly out of focus APE projected image to lead the congregation in a blessing. "Amen," everyone said when the long prayer was finished.

Bob scraped the "moderate" indicator tab on the blue cube container cover with a fingernail, waited while molecular heating elements warmed his lunch, and then opened the package. Blanche did the same before starting on her cube. In a hurry, the pastor scraped "neutral" and removed the cover straightaway.

"Why the hurry, Rev.?" Blanche asked.

"I don't want to miss the smells. It's almost two o'clock."

"I stopped going," Bob lamented. "They made my stomach hurt, and I started feeling really down."

"I've never heard of the smells," Blanche said quizzically. Having only recently relocated to Rockmart, she wasn't familiar with all of the city's attractions. "What are they?"

"Well, no one really knows for sure, but they come every week," Rev. Lacuna explained quietly. Looking around nervously, he continued "They make a lot of people uncomfortable. But if you stand in front of the church between two and three o'clock, the most wondrous odors just appear out of nowhere."

"And there's usually quite a crowd," Bob added.

"They do make my stomach hurt," the minister said. "But I think they're worth it."

"You're telling me that some wonderful odor miraculously appears every Sunday afternoon?" Blanche asked. "What exactly is it?"

"What it is, is a miracle, and nothing less. You must smell them for yourself!"

Blanche Whyte and Rev. Lacuna stood outside in front of the church with a crowd of five hundred people, some were members of First Uni-Clep, some from different congregations, and others who were classified as Non-Attenders by the Bio Data Bureau of the county Department of Information Management, Human Assets Division.

"There they are!" a young man yelled excitedly.

At precisely 2:14 the air above the street became filled with the most wondrous of smells. In silence, every person stood on tiptoes with necks stretched and noses pointed to the sky. The object was to get as close to the odors as possible. Heavy breathing was the only sound to be heard. Several people lost their balance and fell.

"It's a miracle," Rev. Lacuna whispered to Blanche. A second later he asked her, "How does your stomach feel?"

"It aches, like it's empty," she said. "But the smells are amazing. Don't you ever wonder where they come from?" Blanche asked.

"No, I don't," he said emphatically. "They just appear. It's a miracle."

"Maybe the odors come from somewhere," she said. "Maybe from over there." Blanche pointed across the very wide avenue.

"No, that's not possible," the minister said sharply. "Things don't make odors anymore." He wondered if Blanche really was a Bio Data Bureau certified Attender.

After two hours the odors started to dissipate, and thirty minutes after that they were all but gone. A few people milled about talking with friends; otherwise, like the smells themselves, the crowd disappeared, leaving the sidewalk empty save for a few discarded hand-held digital bulletin inserts.

That night Blanche Whyte couldn't sleep. While absolutely captivating, the odors had deeply troubled her.

"What could they be?" she wondered.

Feeling restless, Blanche rolled around and around inside her German lighter-than-air mattress, at one point becoming so fidgety she nearly came loose from her moorings.

"They have to come from somewhere," she thought. But Ms. Whyte had no olfactory point of reference upon which she could draw to help her place the smells.

"Lord, help me to understand," she prayed.

The smells did in fact come from somewhere, and that somewhere was flat number 52–161.34-C, home of one Iago Fabra, the patriarch of a family of Cuban Americans who had come to Rockmart from Miami back in February of 2210 (along with everyone else from that now submerged Florida city). Rockmart, home to a mere 500 souls at the beginning of the twenty-third century and now the largest city in Georgia, had been randomly chosen as the federally mandated destination point for the entire population of Miami when rising sea levels made that city uninhabitable.

For more generations than one could count, the Fabras had been famous restaurateurs, first in Havana, then in Miami, and later in Rockmart. Over time, however, the fast-food industry had quite literally gobbled up all of the nation's family-operated eateries. Not satisfied with mere consolidation, the burger and chicken chains of North America also consumed grocers, farms, meat-packing plants, frozen-food companies, chemical factories, condiment refineries, wineries, and package-delivery firms. Eventually the companies became so colossally efficient at the preparation and delivery of food in epic quantities and inexpensively priced that the family restaurant disappeared, becoming an artifact of an inefficient and decentralized past. (Like every other independent restaurateur, the Fabras had to find other ways of bringing home the bacon.) Then, all records of these establishments were intentionally buried under a mountain of corporate and governmental accounting, permitting and zoning records. Recollection became strictly controlled, too.

Yet, tradition within the Fabra family had the tenacious direction and focus of an orbiting comet. Characterized by dogged will and plain stubbornness, this tradition welded the Fabras not just to their ancient recipes but also to their ingredients, which by now had become closely guarded secrets. Like squirrels they hid seeds and seedlings for a variety of plants and herbs: cumin, plantains, beans, rice, peppers, onions, garlic, yuca, and fruta bomba. These they grew in a secret garden a day's journey from Rockmart. Once each week, on Sunday afternoon, the Fabra clan would descend upon the fifty-second floor homestead flat to practice stealthily an art that had been all but lost to the ages.

What Blanche Whyte, Rev. Lacuna, and the rest of the crowd smelled were the aromas from black beans and rice, boliche, maduros, tostones, fried yuca with onions, arroz con pollo, and a dozen other Cuban dishes prepared from the recipes of Fabra generations past.

"I did a lengthy article on those odors in Rockmart," Dr. Oscar Gil said with great pride. Dr. Gil was a professor of sociological inquiry at Uni-Clep Scientifically Psychological Seminary and a leading expert on unexplained religious phenomena. "A fascinating social construct, I dare say."

Blanche Whyte, in one of the professor's remote offices, was meeting with his APE image hoping to understand what made Rockmart smell.

The image continued, "I believe that these odors, and I don't mean this pejoratively, are similar to the past apparitions of the Virgin Mary. That famous one on a Conyers, Georgia, billboard immediately comes to mind."

Blanche was frustrated. "But they are real!" she said emphatically. "I can feel them in my stomach. And I want to get to their source!"

"This is their source," Dr. Gil replied, pointing to his head. "I myself have been one who has smelled. I know."

In the closet-sized office, Blanche started feeling hot and increasingly exasperated. She fanned herself with a folder and unwittingly disturbed Dr. Gil's image for a moment, distorting his next comment.

"I'm arguing with an APE," she said to herself. "I can't believe it."

"Let me repeat myself," the image said as it came back into focus. "Rockmart Smells are a social construct. They exist only within the shared experience of those who believe they exist." He continued, "Their source is an ephemeralogical commonology, imbued with substance through the aspirative hope of the unlearned."

Blanche sat in silence for a moment. She blew at the APE image, disturbing it again.

"I suggest you stop that," Dr. Gil protested. "If not, I shall adjourn."

Blanche saw a small fan on the windowsill and turned it on.

Once again, at a little after 2:00 on a Sunday afternoon, Blanche Whyte was with Revered Dick Lacuna and the customary large crowd in front of First Uni-Clep. She and everyone else were on tip toes, taking in the smells of Rockmart.

"Don't say I didn't warn you," Rev. Lacuna said in a low voice. "Dr. Gil doesn't believe in miracles. Besides that, he's no longer a Bio Data Bureau certified Attender."

"Well, I'm not giving up," Blanche said resolutely.

"Suit yourself," the pastor said, ending the conversation.

Frustrated with her pastor, Blanche surveyed the crowd. She saw young and old, women and men, singles and couples—all kinds of people representing every group imaginable.

"I know the source."

"What?" Blanche said, turning around. "Who said that?"

"I know the source," the voice repeated, in a whisper.

Behind Blanche stood a small, thin man, seemingly quite old. On his tip toes he couldn't have been much taller than five feet. His face was weathered and unshaven, and the suit he wore was clearly from another day and time.

"Can I trust you?" he asked, taking off his plaid driver's cap.

Blanche looked around to see if anyone was listening.

"I'm no APE," he said. "And I can tell you what you're smelling."

"You know the source?" she asked quietly.

"Can I trust you?"

"Why me?" Blanche asked the man.

"I've been watching you," he replied. "Last week and now today. I hear you asking questions."

"You can trust me," she said, trying to sound as reassuring as possible.

"Then, come with me."

His nose high in the air, Rev. Lacuna did not see Blanche leave with the small, mysterious, old thin man.

Blanche Whyte followed the man down several long canyon-like streets, lined with tall, nondescript, neo-Soviet-style apartment blocks. At the Second Four-Square Southern Bapticostal Church, they turned right and stopped in front of a brown sixty-story building. Blanche suddenly realized they had taken a circuitous route that led them to a door across from First Uni-Clep, a dozen yards from where the crowd of smellers were standing.

"We must be cautious," he said looking over his shoulder. "I don't think we were followed."

To the right of the door on the wall was a pad with four hundred and twenty-three security buttons. The old man pressed the one marked 52–161.34-C.

Blanche heard a synthetic voice coming through a small speaker above the pad of security buttons.

"What does Luther share with a robin?" It asked.

"A diet of worms," The old man replied.

There was a beep, the door popped open, and Ms. Whyte and the old thin man entered the building.

"Three Catherines, two Annes, and one Jane," the same synthetic voice repeated.

"Old Henry wed them all," The old man said. He smiled at Blanche. "We must be very, very careful. At the sound of another beep, a narrow gray sound-proof door at the end of a hallway on the fifty-second floor opened. "Follow me," he directed. Blanche and the old man disappeared into the apartment.

Blanche had trouble understanding Iago Fabra. His voice was nearly lost to the jet-like noise created by giant exhaust fans that were sucking steam and smoke from eighteen two-hundred-year-old roaring gas burners. Pots, frying pans, and saucepans holding contents at various stages of being done were placed in seemingly random order on the various fires. Señor Fabra chopped, diced, flipped, stirred, whipped, and pureed, tending to each concoction in a whirlwind of frenetic activity. The large spoons, knives, cleavers, ladles, spatulas, and whisks he brandished swished through the air like flying swords. Blanche had to dodge the stray bits of onion and garlic that flung over his shoulder as well as the sauces that were splattering everywhere.

"Rice, rice, rice," Iago yelled joyously to his son Spinoza, pointing a big wooden spoon at the young man. "Get the rice on. It's time!" Iago was laughing loudly. "Food grows cold awaiting cooked rice," he said to Blanche.

Spinoza ran to the stove with a pot of water, spilling a little on the floor and on Ms. Whyte's shoes as well. When the water started boiling, Señor Fabra's son added the rice and went to prepare the table for the feast.

Raising his wooden spoon into the air, Iago bellowed above the exhaust fans, "The valleys deck themselves with grain; they shout and sing together for joy!" He laughed, sang, and danced, all the while pretending the spoon was a conductor's baton.

When the rice was cooked and all the dishes were complete and arranged on their serving platters, Iago wiped his hands on a white butcher's apron and stood at the kitchen doorway. "Eat family and friends, drink and be drunk with love!!" he declared to everyone.

"Welcome to the source," the old thin man said softly to Blanche. "By the way, my name is Quinas."

"I don't think I can go back," Blanche said to Quinas.

"To the source?" he asked in a surprised voice.

"No, to First Uni-Clep."

"Oh," he replied.

Blanche and Quinas were in a bland-looking, utilitarian elevator heading down from the fifty-second floor.

"I'm tired of those fake APE images and those tasteless cubes," Blanche said, sounding disgusted and angry.

"I myself was an Attender at First Uni-Clep years ago," Qunias said. "It was just as bland back then, too."

The elevator arrived on the ground floor, expelling Blanche and Quinas into a vacant and cavernous lobby. They left the building and stood outside on the street to talk.

"Why have churches gotten like this?" Blanche asked the old thin man.

Quinas pointed to First Uni-Clep across the very wide avenue. The crowd that had assembled for the smells had now mostly dispersed. "They stopped the questions," he said sadly. "That avenue became a barrier that made them an island."

"I don't follow you," Blanche said, feeling confused.

"For what does one ask, or search, or knock when nothing is needed, everything is known, and all is wide open?" Quinas asked her rhetorically.

"Nothing, I guess," she replied.

"Precisely."

Blanche thought for a moment. "Will the Fabras teach me?" she asked. "I want to taste something again."

"You liked those black beans?" Quinas asked with a chuckle in his voice.

"I had no idea food could be so wonderful. No APE could do the things Sr. Fabra does."

"Well, ask Iago. He's no APE."

Blanche looked across the very wide avenue again. In the distance she could see what she thought was Rev. Lacuna talking with someone she didn't recognize. Seconds later a low-cruising passenger craft whizzed by; a breeze from its wake briefly distorted the minister's image.

"My word, that was an APE, too!" Blanche exclaimed.

Quinas smiled. "You know, you can't always trust what you see, can you?" He gently embraced Blanche and bid her farewell. "Let's meet here next Sunday," he said.

"I can't wait to taste what the Fabras cook up," Blanche said.

"Man, that's bleak," Jim said.

"Am I ever depressed," Sarah added.

"Come on, everybody," Ron cried trying to sound cheerful. "We're like sea horses. There's nothing to worry about." Rev. Morgan was feeling quite creative, and he saw this as an opportunity to try out a new sermon illustration.

"Ron, you've lost me," Dave said.

"Our churches, they're like those mommy sea horses," he explained. "I saw them when I took my youth group to the Aquarium in Atlanta."

"What're you talking about?" Jim asked. "You've lost me, too."

"Our churches will be there to carry our faith to the next generation, you know, the way a mommy sea horse carries her babies in a pouch. The faithful remnant will teach the next generation!"

"Mommy sea horses?" Princeton asked, incredulously. "The male sea horse has the pouch."

"Okay, then, daddy sea horses," Ron replied. "I can live with that."

"But aren't sea horses endangered?" Ed Steale asked. "Like those cute little mommy and daddy creatures, your churches are becoming endangered too."

"God can create a big bush from even the smallest, humblest mustard seed," Jim said.

"You Methodists already had a big bush. Now you're shrinking down to a bunch of little shrubs." Ed was getting snippy.

"Okay, okay. Forget the sea horses and the bushes!" Ron wasn't feeling creative anymore, especially now that he had to find a different illustration for next week's sermon.

"I will be thinking a lot about what the old man said and not about sea horses. About 'when nothing is needed, everything is known, and all is wide open.'" Sue was feeling very troubled.

"Dave," Rev. Princeton Newport said. "I'll be next. We Presbyterian pastors take seriously our role as teachers of the Word. We spend long hours learning biblical languages and studying the history of our faith. We climb the soaring heights of speculative theological inquiry and reach deep into the wellspring of the God-breathed human creative genius. We. . ."

"Oh, go on, Princeton!" Dave said. "Let's just hear your story."

"I call my tale, "My Fair Preacher," Princeton said, ignoring Rev. Tucker. "I take as my text a verse I know by heart. It is taken from the Gospel according to Matthew: 'And you shall love the Lord your God with all your heart and with all you soul and with all your mind.' It is that last part of this verse, I am afraid, that some people overlook." He avoided looking at anyone directly. "I begin my tale. I trust you'll understand its source."

My Fair Preacher

He said to him, "You shall love the Lord your God with all your
heart, and with all your soul, and with all your mind.

(MATTHEW 22:37 NRSV)

"YOU ARE A BUNCH of losers!" Bishop Larry Cash said sarcastically. Bishop
Cash was the Senior Pastor, First Apostle, and founder of the independent
Ever Increasing in Abundance Full Life Gospel Tabernacle Cathedral. "Five
years ago, you had a million and a half members, now you're just above a
million."

Presbyterian pastor Ellie Francis was trying not to feel defensive. "Not
exactly, Larry," she said. "Anyway, we're not about numbers." Ellie tried to
put a positive spin on her denomination's shrinking membership. "We're
about making disciples."

"Disciples?" he asked. "Pretty soon all you'll have will be pews!"

"Like your independent churches are so much better, huh?" Ellie replied. She then held her breath. Bishop Cash was her brother, and she didn't
want flock sizes to become a reason to quarrel.

"Well, yeah, we're growing," Larry said boastfully. "We can't expand
our building fast enough. As a matter of fact, we've got a shortage of ministers." He started laughing. "You've got too many preachers and not enough
members for them to preach to!"

"Well, that way we can be selective," she explained. "I mean you don't want just anybody preaching to a congregation. They need seminary training."

"Seminary?" Larry made a snorting sound and playfully punched Mary's shoulder. "You might as well send 'em to a cemetery," he said, laughing even harder.

"Well, I for one think they need to go to seminary. They need Greek and Hebrew, history, theology, psychology and stuff like that."

"That's your problem," Bishop Cash said.

"What do you mean?"

"Look, how do you get folks into church?" he asked rhetorically. "You've gotta entertain them, that's how!"

The arrival of a waiter interrupted the discussion. "May I take your order now?" he asked.

Chad was his name. He was tall and broad-shouldered and had a very strong jaw line. His personality, however, was less defined. Chad was incapable of making a commitment to anything. At twenty-five years of age, he had already managed to break seven engagements, leave four college degrees unfinished, half-paint his apartment twice, and never repair the two-year-old flat tire on his car. His older sister, a partner in a huge Atlanta law firm, thought it a miracle that he was still working at La Fetida's Mexican sidewalk café. At five months it was his longest stay anywhere.

Larry and Ellie grabbed their menus and ordered lunch.

"I feel like a Number 3 today," Larry said to the waiter. Ellie ordered a Number 7. Both took a side order of chips and salsa plus a soft drink.

"Look Ellie," Bishop Cash said, now a little more softly. "I know you Presbyterians mean well. But if you wanna grow, you're goin' about it all wrong."

"And what do you suggest?" Rev. Francis asked.

"Boldness. Shut down your seminaries. Stick your students in a pulpit and teach 'em how to really preach!"

"What about all the stuff they need to know?"

"All they need is a King James Bible and a microphone," Larry declared. He then looked over Ellie's head. "Oh, good, here's lunch!"

Chad was back with their order. "Here ya go, a Number 2 and a Number 7." He placed the meals on the table. "Enjoy!" he said before starting to walk away.

"Wait a minute!" Larry exclaimed. "I thought I asked for a Number 3." He handed his order back to Chad.

"Oh," Chad replied, looking at the plate. "Actually, a 2 is the same thing as a 3, really," he explained. "Cheese, beans, guacamole; they just arrange it differently." He put Larry's plate back on the table. "I guarantee you won't notice any difference."

"Well, in that case," Bishop Cash said, still a little unsure.

Chad then left the table, feeling quite pleased with himself. "I should be selling used tires," he snickered.

"Ellie," Larry said, continuing the conversation. "I need another associate pastor and fast."

"You think I'd wanna work for you?"

"No, of course not," Larry said. "I'm gonna hire our waiter."

"Him?" Ellie asked. "Are you crazy?" She was incredulous. "Tell me you're not serious."

"I am." Bishop Cash leaned forward to avoid being overheard. "That young man's got the look—broad shoulders, tall, he's not bald. And his voice, it's a bit passive but it's got potential."

Ellie shook her head in disbelief. "You're kidding, right?"

"Watch me." Bishop Cash stood up. He saw Chad leaning against the wall near the bathrooms. Larry waved his hand and motioned for the young man to come to their table. When Chad arrived, Larry sat back down.

"You need something?" Chad asked.

"Young man," Larry said. "I've a proposition for you."

"Me?"

"Have you ever thought of joining the ministry?"

"The what?"

"Preaching, my friend," Larry said. "Look, do you believe in God?"

"Well, yeah."

"Saved?"

"Sure." Chad was thinking of the passbook account his grandmother opened for him when he was a kid. He briefly wondered where he had put it.

"You like it here at La Fetida's?" Larry asked.

"Stinks," Chad replied.

"Young man," Bishop Cash said. "I believe God is calling you, right now."

"Right now?" Chad looked around. "I don't hear anything."

"Right now," Larry said, firmly. "You're gonna be a great preacher, and I'm gonna show you how."

Listening to their conversation, Ellie felt disconnected from everything going on around her. "He's nuts. There's something terribly wrong with this," She thought.

"Here's my cell number and e-mail address," Larry said, handing the puzzled Chad a business card. "You contact me first thing tomorrow."

"Tomorrow," Chad said. "I'll call you tomorrow." He put the card in his pocket and walked away.

Larry looked at Ellie and smiled. "Well, I've got my new associate."

"That's it?" Ellie asked. "You don't even know the guy!"

"God gave him the basics," Larry explained. "He can learn everything else from me."

"Yeah, right."

"Give me six months, and I'll make a great preacher out of that man," Larry promised. "I won't fail."

"You're on. You've got six months."

"All he needs now is a doctorate," Bishop Cash told Ellie. It was exactly six months after their fateful luncheon at La Fetida's. "Otherwise, Chad's done with training."

"I thought you told me he hadn't finished college?"

"I'm gonna get him an honorary divinity doctorate," Larry explained. "I think I've got enough in the budget for one."

Larry and Ellie were in the sky box at the Ever Increasing In Abundance Full Life Gospel Tabernacle Cathedral, observing the Sunday morning service already in progress. A butler arrived with a tray of coffee and English muffins. "Thank you, Cabot," Bishop Cash said while a linen napkin was placed on his lap.

"You make a mockery of theological education," Revered Francis said to her brother in a very serious tone. "No matter how much you spend, it'll be cheap."

Undeterred, Bishop Cash continued. "I've got several options. I just don't know which one to go with yet." He then took a bite from one of the muffins. A few crumbs fell from his mouth as he started talking again. "We had a bit of a disagreement over his title, though."

"He didn't like Reverend? It's good enough for us Presbyterians," Ellie asked.

"He liked Cardinal, but I told him it was too Catholic sounding and wimpy."

"So, what are you gonna call him?"

"First Apostle."

"But that's one of your titles."

"I'm getting another one," Larry explained. "I was thinkin' of something like Primate."

"But that's just as Catholic as Cardinal is."

"I know, but it sounds better." Larry turned to his sister. "Shhhh," he said, holding a finger to his lips. "They've just finished reading the Scripture. Chad's up next."

For ten minutes Bishop Cash, Rev. Francis, Cabot the butler, and the fourteen thousand members of the Ever Increasing In Abundance Full Life Gospel Tabernacle Cathedral sat staring at an empty pulpit. Chad was nowhere to be found.

"Cabot," Bishop Cash yelled. "Find that apostle!"

Down in the sanctuary Lieutenant Bishop Fred Fielding started prophesying. With no preacher in the pulpit, it was the only thing he could think to do. First it was about future wars and plagues, then about the upcoming stock market crash, and from there he took off with warnings about rogue satellites, stray meteorites, artificial intelligence, and black holes.

"We can't find him, sir." Cabot was back in the sky box reporting on the search for Chad. "We've organized a search party. If he's here, we'll find him."

"So, is this what you call a great preacher?" Ellie asked sarcastically.

"Oh, be quiet," Bishop Cash replied. "Just keep looking," he ordered Cabot, who then left the sky box.

"You should've left him at La Fetida's."

Back in the sanctuary several dozen people were lying in aisles, slain in the Spirit after hearing Lieutenant Bishop Fielding's apocalyptic vision of an abysmal future.

"Anyway, as you can see, he wasn't missed." Bishop Cash was now standing by the sky box window pointing down to the sanctuary several hundred feet below.

"I don't get the sense you're putting a lot of thought into training your preachers," the Rev. Francis said. She got up from her seat and stood at the window with her brother. She could see thousands of people shouting in unknown tongues, dancing, jumping up and down, and writhing about on the floors.

"You don't get it, do you?" Bishop Cash told her. "It's not about thinking. They come here because it's exciting," he said, pointing to the people below.

"And what about you? I can't believe you go for this stuff."

Bishop Cash faced the window and looked at the crowds below. He thought about her question for several minutes. Turning to her, he said, "I give them what they want."

"And they give you what you want," she replied.

Larry chuckled. "Are you a bit cynical?" he asked.

"No," she said. "I'm not." The Rev. Francis herself was quiet for a few minutes. "I just look at faith differently than you, brother," she said. "That's all."

"What do you mean?" Larry asked.

"Let's leave it at that for today," Ellie replied. "We'll talk about it some other time." She grabbed her coat and headed for the door. "Look, I've gotta go. I'm running a little late for my own service." The Revered Francis and Bishop Cash hugged each other. "I'll see you at Mom's next Saturday," she said. "She's still mad you changed your last name, you know."

"The name Francis wasn't attracting the crowds we needed. My market people said it was too tranquil sounding," he replied. "Anyway, I'm sorry about Chad. You would've enjoyed his preaching."

"At least you don't have to go and buy him a doctorate."

"Ha, ha." was the last thing Ellie heard her brother say as she left the sky box.

"How did two such different people come from the same family?" she thought, heading down the elevator to the parking level. "Unbelievable."

When Ellie got in her car, she waited a while before turning on the ignition. "I like the name Francis," she said quietly. She thought about the gentle saint whose name she bore. "I couldn't care less what Larry's marketers think. I'm proud of that name."

She started up her car, drove out of the parking lot, and headed to her church for the 11:00 service.

"Princeton's got a good point," Revered Moyers said. "There's anarchy with too much free-wheeling independence."

"Thank you, Sue," Princeton replied feeling vindicated. "The mind can be useful." He pointed to his head.

"Oh, Princeton!" Ed Steale declared. "It's not your brain power that some folks find irksome. It's the way you remind everybody about it all the time."

"Ed!" Rev. Newport shot back. "It's not your shortage of brain power that others find irksome. It's the way you remind everybody about it all the time!"

"Whoa, there," Rev. Tucker cried. "let's cool off a little."

"Ecumenical," Ron reminded everyone. "We must remain ecumenical."

"I apologize," Princeton said contritely. "I was way out of line."

"If I might get back to the point of Princeton's story," Rev. Sue Moyers said. "I can really identify with Ellie Francis. I feel like I have to compete for worshipers with preachers who are not well prepared, who don't know the Bible in depth, nor understand much about theology."

"Is that ever the truth!" Rev. Priestly said in agreement. "Some of those independent ministers will go to any extent to get more people in the door. I heard about one church that was serving coffee and sodas during worship."

"I'd never do something like that," Rev. Steale said, getting a little defensive.

"I didn't mean you, Ed," Sarah said.

"I think my prayer for harmony should have been a bit longer," Dave said, cutting off the discussion. "Hey, I'm ready for another tale!"

"Thank you, Dave," Rev. Priestly said. "I'll take that as my cue." Sarah carefully made her way up to the front of the bus. "Did not our Lord say, 'The greatest among you shall be your servant?'" She asked. "Sometimes it's the least among us that God uses to point this out and that is what my tale is about. I call it, "Thus Spoke Sarah Brewster."

Thus Spoke Sarah Brewster

The greatest among you shall be your servant.

(MATTHEW 23:11 NRSV)

REV. LUCIUS KYLE LOVES the perks that come with being the pastor of the largest, oldest, and most historic church in Cedar Springs. He gets a free copy of the weekly *Cedar Springs Spigot* delivered to his parsonage. The first soda fountain booth at Grady's Apothecary has what pharmacist Lamar Grady calls an eternal reservation for Rev. Kyle. Wheeler's Grocery Store gives him a 15 percent discount on all purchases. He can drive as fast as he wants without getting a ticket, and he can fish anywhere between Cedar Springs and Jakin without needing a fishing license. And in the Veteran's Memorial Assembly Hall at council meetings, plays, and concerts, Lucius always gets the coveted center chair in the first row. But the one perk Rev. Lucius Kyle likes above all is the loud siren and whirling cherry-red emergency roof light with which his official-church-use car is outfitted.

Until recently, like most folks in Cedar Springs, twelve-year-old Sarah Brewster never gave Rev. Lucius Kyle a second glance when she saw him whizzing down Wide Street with his siren screaming and his light spinning.

"You kinda get used to 'im," Lamar Grady told his mother-in-law last time she drove all the way from Waycross to visit.

"Don't give it much thought," grocer Houston Wheeler always replied when asked. "I guess old Rev. Kyle's up to a lot of really important stuff."

Lately, however, young Sarah Brewster was beginning to find Rev. Kyle more than just a nuisance.

"Mom," she cried at breakfast one Monday morning before school. "It's not fair."

"Rev. Kyle is an important man in Cedar Springs, dear." Sarah's mother Janet replied. "Folks need him."

"It still ain't fair."

"Don't use that word. Besides, you and Amy didn't know you were sittin' in the Reverend's booth. That's why Mr. Grady asked you to move," she explained calmly. "Now you do know."

"But we had to wait an hour for another place to sit!" Sarah complained.

"I'm sure it wasn't that long. Besides, Reverend Kyle has important things to do. Visiting folks in the hospital, stuff like that," she said. "He can't be late 'cause, like I said, folks need him."

"Hmmf," Sarah muttered. She got up from the table, grabbed her bookbag and lunchbox, and headed for school.

"Class, open your books to page fifteen." civics teacher Lisa Colquit told her students.

Dutifully, with one or two exceptions, the eleven middle-school children flipped through the pages of their textbooks, stopping at page fifteen.

"Class, can anyone tell me something about the Bill of Rights?" A long period of silence followed. Feeling frustrated, she continued. "This chapter was your homework assignment. Surely somebody knows something." There was more silence. John Bradshaw then raised his hand.

"Oh good, finally somebody," she thought. "Yes, John."

"Miss Colquit, may I go to the bathroom?"

Lisa found teaching civics to middle schoolers exasperating. Aside from changes in clothing and hair styles, each year was always the same. With the county seat of Blakely nearly an hour away, the state capitol Atlanta several more, and Washington, D.C. even further, Ms. Colquit had a hard time getting her students connected with the subject. "If they'd only call it something else," she often thought. "Anything but civics."

"Ms. Colquit," Sarah called out, vigorously raising her hand.

"Yes, Sarah, do you need to go to the bathroom, too?"

"No, Ma'am," Sarah replied. "I have a question about the First Amendment."

Lisa couldn't believe her ears! This was the first Constitution-related question she had entertained from a student since at least Bill Clinton was

President. "What's your question?" she asked, starting to feel hope stir just a little.

"It says here, 'Congress shall make no law respecting an establishment of religion.' Does that mean Rev. Kyle shouldn't get first dibs on the best booth at Grady's?"

"Huh?" Lisa asked. Her spirit quickly sank back. "I don't follow you," she said.

"Rev. Kyle, Ma'am," Sarah explained. "If someone's sitting in the first booth at Grady's soda fountain and then Rev. Kyle comes in, they gotta move. Does this mean that's against the constitution?"

"Well, no," Ms. Colquit replied. "At least it's a question. I should be thankful for that," she mused. She continued, "It's a store policy. It wasn't a law the Cedar Springs council voted on. And technically it's not discriminating according to Federal law, either."

"But it's not fair," Sarah complained.

"That may be the case, but it's not unconstitutional."

Seeing that there were no more questions, Lisa Colquit proceeded with her annual Bill of Rights lecture. As always, not for a minute did she believe that any of her students would take its message to heart.

This year she was wrong.

Walking home from school, Sarah pondered the Bill of Rights and especially that First Amendment. "Rev. Kyle's gotta be unconstitutional, somehow," she said to herself.

Lost in thought, Sarah almost didn't notice Lucius zip by. Approaching the town's only intersection with a traffic light, the minister flipped on his red light and siren, startling Sarah. Suddenly looking up, she watched him run the red light, smack in front of Sheriff Barker, who in turn smiled at Lucius and waved.

Sarah crossed the street and walked up to the sheriff. "Why didn't you give him a ticket?" she asked, crossly. She pointed down the street at the vanishing minister.

"Why, young lady, that was Rev. Kyle," he explained, not used to having his authority challenged, least of all by a girl in middle school. "He doesn't get tickets."

"Why not?"

"Well, uh, he just doesn't."

"You already said that, Sir." Sarah was feeling miffed at not being taken seriously. "I don't understand why you treat him differently."

"'Cause he's Rev. Kyle." Sheriff Barker was getting impatient with Sarah. "Why are you askin' so many questions?"

"'Cause I don't think it's fair. That's what I think!"

"You should go home, young lady," Sheriff Barker said. "And that's what I think!"

"Hmmf," Sarah muttered. Continuing her trek home, she walked past Grady's Apothecary. She got even angrier when she recalled being bumped out of the first booth. She passed Wheeler's Grocery Store and then the Bank of Cedar Springs, where she almost walked into Mayor Fogg, who had just finished a financial transaction. Next, she turned up Magnolia Street and walked the final block to her home.

"Mom!" she yelled, entering the house through the open kitchen door. "I saw Rev. Kyle run the red light, and Sheriff Barker did nothing about it." The oven was on, and the outside door had been left wide open in an attempt to dissipate some of the heat it created.

"Honey," her mom replied. "He must have been on the way to the hospital."

"Yeah, but he ran the red light!"

"Somebody must have needed him really bad."

"Yeah, but that's not constitutional!"

"That's not what?" Her mother asked, puzzled. Janet Brewster was preparing dinner and had been only partly attentive to the conversation. She dropped her paring knife on the cutting board and faced Sarah. She wiped her hands on her apron.

"Unconstitutional, Mom. He's supposed to get a ticket, just like everybody else. It says so in the Bill of Rights."

"And where did you learn that?"

"Ms. Colquit," Sarah said. "She told us all about our Bill of Rights in civics today. It says the government can't make laws that respect religion."

"I'm sure that doesn't apply to Rev. Kyle," Mrs. Brewster said. "Now go wash up for dinner."

"Hmmf," Sarah muttered. She marched upstairs to her bedroom. There she tossed her bookbag on the bed, changed her clothes, and then headed to the bathroom to wash her hands.

Saturday morning found Sarah at Wheeler's Grocery store. She was there to buy a gallon of milk and a box of cereal.

"Hey, wait a minute!" Sarah exclaimed. "Don't I get more change?" she asked Houston Wheeler. By chance Rev. Kyle had just purchased the same amount of milk and an identical box of cereal. Distrustful of the minister, she had watched his transaction like a suspicious IRS agent. Sarah held her hand out for more money.

"That's all you're due, young lady," Mr. Wheeler said.

"I gave you a five, just like Rev. Kyle," she explained. "But you gave him more change."

"That's 'cause he gets a discount." Like Sheriff Barker, Houston did not appreciate being challenged, especially by the likes of a girl attending middle school. "Now go home."

"That's not fair, Mr. Wheeler," Sarah continued, not wanting to drop the subject. "I want the same thing Rev. Kyle got."

"Rev. Kyle is an important man in our town."

"I still don't think it's fair. Why should he pay less than I do?"

"Cause he's a minister and you're not. Now go home."

"Hmmf," Sarah muttered. She marched out of the store, stomping her feet on the old wooden floors and making as much noise as possible. Outside, she saw Lucius leaving the store parking lot. The minister flipped on his siren and whirling red light and sped through the town's intersection. Sheriff Barker waved as Rev. Kyle ran the red light. Sarah shook her head and walked on home.

"Mom," she yelled, entering the house through the kitchen door. The screen door slapped against its wooden frame. "Did you know Mr. Wheeler gives Rev. Kyle a discount?" She put the milk in the ice box and placed her cereal in the pantry.

"Well, dear, Rev. Kyle is a minister."

Sarah handed her mother the change from her purchase. "There'd be more if I were a minister," she said sarcastically.

"Rev. Kyle does a lot for our town, and we've got to support him any way we can."

Despite her mother's explanations, despite everything Mr. Wheeler and Mr. Grady had said, and despite Sheriff Barker's reasoning, Sarah was not buying any of it.

"No," she thought. "It's not fair."

"Yes, young lady," Mayor Hugh Fogg said. "You have the floor."

It was Monday night, and Sarah was at the monthly meeting of the Cedar Springs City Council at the Veterans Memorial Assembly Hall. The mayor and the town's four elected representatives sat on the stage in metal chairs arranged around a laminated folding table. Sarah had been waiting patiently to speak and was now standing at the wooden lectern and microphone in the middle of the room, just in front of the first row.

"My name's Sarah Brewster," she began. To reach the microphone, she had to balance herself on top of an upturned metal bucket taken from the custodian's utility closet. "I attend Cedar Springs Middle School, and I live on Magnolia Street with my mom."

"Miss Brewster," Mayor Fogg said. "We're delighted you're here." Addressing the audience he continued. "I think it's a fine thing when our young people take an interest in our town's government."

"Thank you, Sir," Sarah replied.

"Now what seems to be on your mind young lady?"

"Mayor Fogg, ladies and gentlemen of the council, citizens of Cedar Springs," she began respectfully in the style she memorized from her civics textbook. "I've got here my copy of the Bill of Rights." She shook her rolled-up reproduction of the eighteenth century document in the air.

Mayor Fogg, the council, Rev. Kyle, and the citizens of Cedar Springs all laughed.

"How cute," Rev. Kyle whispered to Houston Wheeler who was seated next to him.

"I'm pleased someone as young as yourself is taking such an interest in history," Mayor Fogg said to Sarah. "Especially since Memorial Day's coming up real soon."

"Thank you, Mr. Mayor, Sir," Sarah said. "Like I was saying. I've got here my copy of the Bill of Rights. It says y'all are improperly showing favors to Rev. Kyle." She turned around and bravely pointed to Lucius. "It ain't fair, and I think it should stop," Sarah said, a little sharply. She turned around to the stone-faced Mayor Fogg and town council members. No one uttered a word. "It's unconstitutional; that's what it is."

"I'm sure you'll make a fine lawyer one day, Miss Brewster," Mayor Fogg said patronizingly. "There's nothing in that document that says we can't show a little appreciation to our Rev. Kyle." The members of the council all smiled and nodded their heads.

Sarah dug her toes into the insoles of her shoes. She gripped the side of the lectern so firmly that the veins in her hands were visible, even to people seated in the fourth row. She put on her glasses and looked nervously at the mayor. "Actually, Sir," she replied. "There is."

For Mayor Fogg this particular town council meeting was his formal introduction to the wondrous power the Internet has bestowed upon a new technologically driven and fully wired generation. For two solid weeks, each day after school, Sarah had surfed the Web, foraging through everything known to humankind on the topic of church-state relations. And one evening, in the on-line law library of the University of the Oklahoma Pan Handle, she found what she needed. It was the obscure case of the United States of America vs. the Rev. Hubert G. Craggert and the First Church of Glakoma, Oklahoma.

Like Rev. Kyle of Cedar Springs, Hubert G. Craggert was the senior pastor of his town's most important church. Rev. Craggert, too, enjoyed hundreds of legal and social perks, from traffic regulation exemptions to discounts on fishing tackle. And like Lucius, Hubert loved the siren and whirling light that equipped his church car. Yet unlike Lucius, Hubert's perks caught the eye of the U.S. Attorney's office in Oklahoma City. In 1934 a suit was filed in federal court that ultimately brought his perks to an abrupt end.

"I rest my case," Sarah finally said. She had just finished reading the entire fifty-three page, legal-sized-paper transcript from the United States of America versus Rev. Hubert G. Craggert and the First Church of Glakoma, Oklahoma. Mayor Fogg had tried several times to interrupt Sarah, but like a retriever digging a hole, she wouldn't stop until she got to what she thought was making the smell. And that, in her mind, was the clear and indisputable fact that Cedar Springs was, indeed, respecting the establishment of religion.

Unbeknownst to Sarah, seated in the rear of the Veterans Assembly Hall was her mom and her Civics teacher. Both Janet Brewster and Lisa Colquit stood up and cheered.

Several Saturdays later, Sarah was leaving Wheeler's Grocery store with a gallon of milk and a dozen eggs. She stepped into the bright South Georgia sunlight and onto a very hot sidewalk. When her eyes finally adjusted to the light, she saw Sheriff Barker on the other side of the street. He was talking to Rev. Kyle who was seated at the wheel of his car, which now had several pieces of electrical tape covering a large hole on the top where his whirling red emergency light had once sat. Then she noticed the Sheriff rip a long pink slip of paper from a booklet and hand it to a clearly angry Lucius.

"I wonder what that was all about," she thought.

She continued her trek up Wide Street, passed Grady's Apothecary, and turned the corner at Magnolia, and ran the final block home.

"Mom!" Sarah yelled. "I'm home!"

"Hi," Mrs. Brewster replied, smiling at her daughter.

"Mom, you ever wonder why Mayor Fogg goes to the bank so often?"

"Well, I guess he must have a lot of financial transactions to make."

"Boy, I'll say. He goes there at least every day, and sometimes two or three times."

"He's an important man, dear," Janet said. "Now why don't you go get ready for lunch."

"Humph," she muttered." Sarah ran upstairs to the bathroom. She washed her hands and dried them on an old towel that once belonged to her grandmother. Looking into the mirror, she said to herself, "I'll bet that Mayor Fogg's up to something unconstitutional."

"Whoa! What's that noise?" Rev. Sarah Priestly asked nervously. An ear-splitting grinding sound was coming from the bottom of the bus.

"I hope that's not our transmission," Ron yelled, trying to be heard over the loud noise.

"Dave, maybe you should have prayed harder for our bus!" Rev. Jim Mayer shouted.

"I'm not worried. It'll hold out till we get to Camp Candleberry." But just as Dave tried to keep everybody calm, the transmission gave off one final loud clunk and then fell to the ground. The bus coasted to a stop on the narrow shoulder, about a dozen yards from where various gear parts, metal chips, and oily fluids had hit the roadway.

"I think you should've added a prayer for our safety," Ron said anxiously as the wake of a motor coach taking a group of Catholic bishops to Rock City sped by, shaking their bus.

"We'd better find some help," Jim suggested. He, too, was anxious.

"Princeton, don't you have a cell phone?" May asked.

"That's right!" Rev. Newport said, perking up. Suddenly, everyone's mood rose, and hope filled the air. "I have it right here." He reached for his belt pouch. Not finding it, he started looking all around his seat. "Now where did I put it?"

"You mean that fancy 5G one with email and internet connection you went on and on about back at breakfast?" Sarah asked.

"Yes, I had it with me this morning."

"You mean the one with global positioning?" Jim asked.

"The one with artificial intelligence?" Sue asked.

"Yes, that's the one," Princeton said with some pride.

"It's back at Sam's Diner!" Jim said.

Now embarrassed, Princeton stopped searching and everyone else's mood descended to a new low. Several curious buzzards started circling above the bus. Two of them landed on the roof, hoping something unfortunate would soon transpire.

"It's pretty dark out there," Rev. Billy Barker said. "You can't see a darn thing."

"I don't think we should go out anywhere," Rev. Bob Bending added. "It's probably not safe."

"Yeah, we'd better stay put," Ben Boyle agreed.

"How far from Camp Candleberry do you think we are?" Sarah asked Dave.

"Well, I'm not exactly sure. I kinda lost track of how far we've come."

"Maybe they'll send out a search party," Ed said

"I'm certain of that," Dave said, though inside he wasn't quite as sure. "All we need to do is to wait here."

"What about your tale, Dave?" Sarah asked. "That'll help us pass the time!" The other ministers cheered in agreement, happy to get their minds off of their hopeless predicament. Dave then got up and with all the confidence he could muster, strode down the aisle to the front of the bus.

"My tale," he began. "I call 'The Boys of Blakely.' It's a story of new beginnings. It takes its cue from Mark 2:22 and it's all about our need for new wineskins."

The Boys of Blakely

And no one sews a piece of unshrunk cloth on an old cloak;
otherwise, the patch pulls away from it, the new from the old,
and a worse tear is made.

(MARK 2:22 NRSV)

"HALLELUJAH!" REV. BOB BUNCH yelled. "Praise the Lord! Thank you, Jesus!" The district superintendent of the Methodist church's Early County district was jumping up and down. The hair he used to cover his bare scalp was now flapping over his left ear. "It's a boy! It's a boy!"

Rev. Jim Tate came running into Bob's office. He had been in the hallway by the coffee machine waiting for this news from their new bishop. Today was May 3, and it was exactly 2:00 pm. The e-mail message from the Southwest Georgia Conference center that had been due at any momentobviously just arrived.

"A boy?" Rev. Tate, Deputy District Superintendent, asked as he entered the office. He'd been nervous all day and wanted assurance that what he thought he had heard was indeed true.

"Man, oh man, a boy!" Bob repeated, unable to hold back his excitement. Half of his shirt was now untucked and hanging over his belt.

Like two peas in a pod, Jim and Bob faced each other. They stomped their feet, then put fists together and grunted like title-hungry rugby players. "Grrrrrrrrrrr!" they growled almost in unison.

"What's his name?" Jim asked.

"Robert," Bob replied. The district superintendent was reading from a spreadsheet attachment file that had accompanied the e-mail. Each column in the spreadsheet provided valuable data about their new minister. "I wonder if they call him Bob like me?"

"What else does it say?" An eager Jim wanted to know.

"Says baptized a Methodist, his parents are from Augusta," Bob read. "Hmm, good he's not from Atlanta," he muttered. "He's a graduate of Free for All Theological Seminary. It says single and likes fishing, football, and footlongs." The District Superintendent looked up at Jim. "He'll fit right in!"

"Boy, I was afraid that the new bishop was gonna send a girl preacher down here," Jim said. "I was sure they were gonna make us change."

"I told the bishop that nobody wanted a woman assigned here," Bob added. "I'm glad they listened to me for a change. Folks in our churches don't like it when a girl does the preaching."

"Yeah," Bob said. "It's not right, and we don't think Jesus wants it that way."

"The e-mail says the bishop's gonna bring the new preacher to our retreat next weekend." Bob continued. "They'll arrive late in the morning on Saturday. It says that'll give us the better part of the day to get to know each other."

"What else does the bishop say?"

"The new preacher's gonna do the annual revival sermon that Sunday at First Church." Bob looked at Jim. "Whew," he said, rubbing his forehead. "I thought I was gonna get stuck doing it." Turning back to the monitor, Bob finished reading the letter. "The bishop wants all the ministers in our district there. It says our new preacher gives one heck of a good sermon and all of us need to hear it."

"What? Don't they think we can preach down here?"

"At least we don't have to listen to a girl!" Bob said with relief.

The clergy from the Early County district always held their annual retreat at the Glory Days Campground, one of the larger campsites within the Methodist Retreat Center complex. It sat right next to Lake Jericho which in addition to providing recreation for several generations of ministers, also serves as a reservoir for the nearby town of Cedar Springs.

Camp Glory Days was the furthest campsite from the parking lot, four and a half miles by way of a pea-gravel roadway that was too narrow for anything wider than a moped. The road took a winding route through a steep wooded dale and across two dry creek beds before opening onto Lake Jericho's wide artificial beach. The bishop and the new minister had parked their car and were making that long trek, pulling their wheeled luggage behind them, which was bouncing over every exposed tree root and rock.

"It won't be easy for you here, by any stretch of the imagination," the bishop said.

"I'm glad I'll meet them on this retreat. It's different when you're in these natural elements."

"Don't get your hopes up too much. I understand folks 'round here don't take kindly to change."

"Well, I'll look for things we have in common. Underneath, we're not so different."

"I don't think they'll see it that way," the bishop said, unconvinced.

"Look, I've been praying about my appointment for weeks now. I believe I'm ready for whatever I have to face," the new preacher replied.

"I don't doubt that. I just hope you don't have to face too much."

The unofficial highlight of the annual minister's retreat was a morning of skinny-dipping in Lake Jericho. To those involved, skinny-dipping was a great bonding experience and a powerful way to break free of inhibitions. At the same time, however, this tradition could continue only because the clergymen of the Early County District had successfully avoided breaking down an even bigger barrier, namely that of sex.

The South Georgia Conference center offices had a big barrier too: namely Sandra McGerney, the self-conscious, far-sighted administrator. Everyone knew she needed reading glasses, but she just couldn't bring herself to buy them. This had never presented a problem for anyone until now. Neither Bob nor Jim nor any of the Methodist ministers in Early County were aware that the new preacher's name had one additional letter that Sandra had overlooked. The preacher that they all thought was named Robert and a "he" was actually named Roberta and was a "she."

The four-and-a-half-mile hike from the parking lot to Camp Glory Days afforded the new bishop and Roberta a lot of time to work on a strategy. They both knew that breaking the district's sex barrier would be tough, and they braced themselves for what would be a very uncomfortable first meeting. The long walk also provided enough time for the Bob and Jim plus the ten Methodist preachers of Early County to strip off their clothes and jump into Lake Jericho.

"Man, oh man, why didn't they make him get a haircut?" Bob muttered to Jim when he realized the bishop and the new preacher had just arrived. Because his glasses were resting on his pile of clothes several yards away, Roberta was not in focus.

"Mind if we join you?" the bishop hollered to everyone in the lake

"Man, oh man," Jim whispered back to Bob. "That ain't no man!"

"Where can we change?" Roberta yelled.

"Man, oh man," Bob said to Jim, suddenly looking all around. He was panicking. "Where's all the water going?" Sure enough, every one of the skinny-dipping Early County ministers could feel the cool chill of air against an ever-increasing portion of their bare skin.

Fred Thompson from the Cedar Springs Public Works Department could not have chosen a more inopportune morning to bring down the walls of Jericho dam. Yes, he did need to drain the lake for its overdue annual spring cleaning. But the superintendents and the ten stark-naked Methodist preachers would gladly have taken on an army of Massachusetts Unitarians had they been able to pick an alternate day.

Bob, Jim, and the other clergymen grabbed the only covering within reach: kudzu leaves that were growing on a lush vine covering a bank to their immediate right.

The next day nearly a thousand folks from every nook and cranny of Early County showed up for the annual First Methodist Church May revival, an increase over the previous year by a factor of at least four. Indeed, this crowd was the largest ever, for many folks had come to see what a woman preacher looked like. People filled that church: The center aisle of the sanctuary as well as the back row and narthex were replete with folding chairs. A lot of folks were even sitting on the steps to the balcony and standing outside on ladders that they had leaned against the open windows.

District Superintendent Bob and Deputy District Superintendent Jim were in the first row, along with the new bishop and the other ten Methodist preachers of Early County.

"I'll bet it's gonna be one of those touchy-feely sermons," a sarcastic Jim whispered to Bob. He sat with his legs crossed and arms folded across his chest (as did most everyone else in the first row). "I hate touchy-feely sermons." The kudzu had left an irritating rash that had put him in a real bad mood. This was on top of feeling utterly humiliated.

"Watch her quote some stupid poem," Bob replied. He, too, had a rash. Sitting on a hard wooden pew did not help.

Roberta, in contrast, sat comfortably near the altar in one of the large white cushioned chairs. She was, however, feeling a little peculiar and was desperately trying to clear her mind of all images from Saturday. When it was time for Scripture to be read, Roberta climbed into First Church's high pulpit. The lectionary text for that Sunday was unfortunate and made Roberta even more tense. She opened to the book of Genesis in the large and historic King James Bible that had been used by this congregation for over one hundred and fifty years.

"And the eyes of them both were opened," Roberta read in the most commanding voice she could muster. "And they knew that they were naked. . ."

Roberta stopped reading and blushed. She looked down at Bob and Jim, who were also blushing and still sitting with their legs crossed. She then started laughing. She knew the text spoke of Adam and Eve and had universal application to human sin and rebellion. Yet for Roberta (and for that matter, Jim, Bob, and everybody on the first row), on this Sunday evening, the text also pointed to the previous day's events at Lake Jericho.

Roberta took a deep breath and continued reading, ". . .and they sewed fig leaves together and made aprons." Roberta again looked at Bob and Jim, who were looking at their laps. She then thought of the kudzu leaves. She couldn't stop laughing. She tried taking another deep breath. She tried drinking a little water from the glass in the pulpit. She even tried pinching her wrist. Nothing worked.

"I can't take this anymore," Bob muttered to the bishop. "I've gotta go home and hide." He inched his way down the pew and fled through a side door. Then, one by one, Jim and the other Methodist ministers of Early County likewise left the First Church sanctuary via that same door.

"I better salvage this mess," the bishop thought. He then got up and walked to the pulpit. "Why don't you sit down," he told Roberta.

"Okay," she replied, still laughing hard.

The bishop stepped up to the old King James Bible to finish reading the Scripture text: "And Adam and his wife hid themselves from the presence of the LORD."

This time the bishop was the one unable to continue reading. Looking at the now empty first row, he chuckled. The chuckle quickly turned into uncontrollable laughter. He excused himself, telling the congregation he would be right back.

Several years later, on a fine Saturday morning the bishop came calling upon Roberta who was still ministering in Blakely. As a matter of fact, she now had quite a following. Several other women were preaching in the Early District too.

"Good ole Jim and Bob wanted you back in Augusta," he told Roberta.

"I haven't thought about those two for months. Whatever happened to them?"

"Bob's got himself a church pretty far up north."

"Where?"

"North Pole, Alaska," the bishop said.

"Now he's as frozen in body as he is in time!"

"What about Jim? What's he up to?"

"He's a chaplain for some scientists."

"Scientists?" Roberta asked. "You put him at a university?"

"Not quite. The Board of Global Ministries sent him to a research station."

"Where?"

"You'll never guess."

"Tell me, where?"

"Antarctica."

"Our peas-in-a-pod are now poles-apart!" Roberta laughed.

"I was sure surprised how fast things changed around here," the bishop said. "No one ever thought it would happen."

"We sure had some barriers we had to get through, though."

"Yes," the bishop said. "But we had help from the Public Works people."

"Their timing was unbelievable," Roberta noted. "They couldn't have picked a worse day to drain the lake."

"Or a better day," the bishop countered. "The walls of Jericho had to come down sometime."

"If you ask me, I say our ole bus needs a new wineskin," Rev. Priestly said to Dave.

"What do you mean?" he asked, a little confused.

"You should've invested in a new transmission when you got the thing," Sarah explained. "I think it needed more than your church's name on it."

"Well, I was aiming to get it fixed," Dave replied, feeling defensive. "I just never got around to it."

"You definitely should've had some real prayer warriors lay hands on that transmission this morning," Ed added.

"Prayer warriors?" Sarah cut in. "A simple mechanic would've been better."

"Look, I'm certain the folks at Camp Candleberry will be along soon," Dave said, hiding his growing uncertainty.

"Anyway," Sarah continued. "Your story really hit home for me. I think it brought us full circle. "Our faith is always transformative, not simply a conversion."

"Each one of us has had to cross a barrier at some point," Dave replied.

"Like the barrier of ignorant men," Sue said sarcastically. "It was really tough for me when I started in the ministry. All the good ole boys wanted me to go away."

"Ditto," Sarah exclaimed. "A whole bunch of folks, men and women alike, didn't want me around either."

"I think we're simply afraid of change, that's all," Rev. Ron Morgan noted. "Wasn't it Paul who said the only thing we've got to be afraid of is being afraid?"

"Paul?" Dave asked. "I don't think Paul said that."

"It was President Roosevelt," Sue said.

"And I think it was fear itself that we had to fear," Princeton added.

"What does this have to do with barriers, anyway?" May asked.

"Fear makes us put up barriers," Ron said. "That's what I mean."

"This is at the heart of our transformation," Dave added.

"That darkness outside is a good enough barrier for me," Rev. Ed Steale said, putting his coat on to keep warm. "We're going nowhere."

"That's for sure," Ben, Billy, and Bob added simultaneously.

"On that note," Dave said. "I'm gonna try to get some sleep."

"Me, too!" Sue Moyers had covered herself with her coat and was trying to get comfortable on one of the bench seats.

"Before we sleep, I want to repeat something Bob said about the Bible that I thought was very inciteful. He said, 'It's too big for anybody.' Tell us what you mean by that," Dave asked.

"First, I feel you gotta be part of a community of disciples, both with the living and with those who went before us, going all the way back to the Apostles. There's been 2,000 years of bible studies, sermons, church services, missions, and creeds. We can't ignore our shared history, both the good and all too often, bad. Second, the Bible is complex, even the Gospels. Not naming any names, but a lot of people out there believe they got the only right interpretation. Unfortunately, this is more common than not."

"So true! Instead of following our Savior, we try to make him a follower of us," Sarah felt very passionate about what she just said.

"No matter how often you pray or how much education you have, and even if you think God speaks to you directly, no one person or group can grasp the whole thing by themselves," Billy added.

"Good, I think we got it," Ron said. "Now I really need to sleep on it.

"On that note, good night. Our community of believers is very tired," Dave said, ending the conversation.

Epilogue

"HEY! WHAT'S THAT NOISE?" Rev. Ron Morgan cried. He jumped up and banged his head on the metal luggage rack just above the seats. It was nearly 10:00 in the morning and the twelve ministers were only now waking up from a night of fitful sleep aboard the old bus.

"Shhhh," Rev. Moyers whispered. "Somebody's knocking at the door!" All the pastors except Dave ducked behind the psychedelic seats.

"That's Jenny Sales, the new camp director," Rev. Tucker said, rubbing his eyes. He felt a sudden surge of relief. "They must have come looking for us after all!" Sensing no immediate danger, the other ministers peered over the backs of the seats.

"Thank you, God!" Princeton was looking upwards; his praying hands looked just like those in the famous Dürer etching. Then, one by one the O'Postles arose and looked around.

"Am I ever hungry," Ron Morgan added. "Last night I dreamed about bacon, buttermilk biscuits, pancakes, grits, juice, and, oh, yes, coffee." He was rubbing his stomach and envisioning a breakfast feast.

"I myself could go for a big bowl of oatmeal," Ken Lesley said.

"Not grainy gruel? Sue joked.

Dave pushed the door open and greeted Jenny. This frightened the two buzzards that had been asleep on top of the bus. Their wings slapped and banged against the roof as they got themselves airborne and flew away. The camp director then stepped into the bus to greet the tired and stiff Early County clergy.

"Good God, it stinks in here," she said, shaking her head. "It's so stuffy. Why on earth did y'all spend the night in here?"

"We were stuck," Dave replied, stating what he thought should have been obvious. "Our bus broke down."

"We dropped the transmission back yonder." Ron pointed to the pile of bus parts sitting in the highway about a dozen yards behind them. "We couldn't go anymore."

"My word! Look at those mountains over there!" Sarah cried. She was looking outside at the terrain around them.

"Those are the mountains of Chattooga," Jenny replied proudly, as though she had something to do with their being there.

"Uh, oh," Sue Moyers said. "Look over there!" She was the first to see a small wooden sign a few yards away. It marked the entrance to a gravel driveway.

"Oh, my word!" Ron also noticed the sign. "Dave, you'd better come have a look."

Now it was Dave's turn to look out the front window. "No!" he cried. "It can't be!"

Not more than twenty yards ahead stood the welcome sign for Camp Candleberry; their cabins could not have been more than a quarter mile further.

"We were about to send out a search party," Jenny said, "but Roy saw you and the bus when the search party got started. He texted me that your bus was stopped right outside our gate and that y'all were on board, safe and sound."

"Why didn't he come in and get us?" Sarah was flabbergasted.

"Yeah!" Ron added. "Why not?"

"He was fixing to! He kept knocking on your door," Jenny told every-one. "You were carryin' on so much that he couldn't get your attention."

"Well, I for one am very hungry," Ed declared.

"Yeah, me, too," Billy and Bob said in unison. Ben stuck a thumb in the air to indicate his agreement.

"When do we get breakfast?" Ron asked. "I hope you've got some pan-cakes and bacon."

"Or oatmeal," Ken added.

"I'm so sorry," Jenny said. "Breakfast was over thirty minutes ago. Y'all missed it."

"Isn't there something left for us to eat?" Ron was starting to whine.

"Well, we've got gobs of communion wafers you can have, plus, some jelly."

"Communion wafers?" Jim asked, "That's all you've got?"

"Staff here love to dip them in humus," Jenny replied. The bus got very quiet again. "Can I tell Roy to toast 'em for you, with a little cheese on top, maybe?" she asked.

"Gosh, no, Jenny," Dave replied for everyone. "We appreciate the offer, but don't go fussing around on our account." Ben, Billy, and Bob nodded their heads. So did everyone else this time.

"Something seems sacrilegious about this," May Presley muttered.

"I wasn't that hungry, anyway," Ken said.

"We neither," Ben, Billy, and Bob said together.

"Suit yourselves. Anyway, our Roy will fix up some pizza for lunch. I think you'll love it." Jenny was trying very hard to be positive.

"Pizza?" May asked. "What kind?"

"Well, mini pizza's, actually."

"Mini pizza?" Dave asked. "What, are they just real small?"

"They're really micro pizzas," Jenny clarified.

"Micro pizzas?"

"Yeah, we use those old communion wafers."

"Something is seriously out of order here," May muttered.

"Like I said, we've got millions of them. Add tomato sauce and some cheese and they're actually quite nourishing and yummy."

www.ingramcontent.com/pod-product-compliance
Lightning Source LLC
Chambersburg PA
CBHW051140020726
47501CB00005B/1595